"A menagerie of hungry familiars perfectly paired with rich, evolving bouquets. From Asti to Reisling, Williams pours her readers into the sprawling branches of *Penfold's Menu of Magic and Malice*. Intoxicating!" - **L. E. Daniels, Shirley Jackson and Bram Stoker Award® finalist, author of *Serpent's Wake: A Tale for the Bitten***

"Each story a delectable taste, Valerie Williams delivers a fine menu of fiction whimsical and dark, funny and sad. Each story brings its own contribution to a most enjoyable palate." - **Patrick Freivald, Bram Stoker Award® finalist**

"From haunted heirlooms to sinister swamp cryptids, *Penfold's Menu of Magic and Malice* will satisfy your appetite for horror and leave you craving more. It's easy to see

why Valerie B. Williams is sought after by many a curator of short stories; prepare to savor every page of her latest."
- **Christa Carmen, author of *The Daughters of Block Island* and *How to Fake a Haunting***

"With her stylish narrative voice, Valerie Williams brings you a delicious assortment of frights (complete with wine pairings). With its courses rooted in history, mythology, childhood nightmares, and pure adult dread, *Penfold's Menu of Magic and Malice* will satiate your cravings but likely leave you hungry for more. The perfect option for late-night when you're feeling peckish." - **Stephen Mark Rainey, author of *The House at Black Tooth Pond, Fugue Devil Resurgence, The Nightmare Frontier,* and many others**

"Valerie Williams creates a feast of fear with course after course of monsters and mayhem. Her voice is clear and her knife is sharp. This collection deserves a place on every horror reader's shelf." - **Donna J. W. Munro, author of the *Poppet Cycle Series***

"Add three parts of scares and a dash of wicked fun for *Penfold's Menu of Magic and Malice*, a culinary delight of Horror tales for sinister, ghastly, and gruesome palates." - **Eric J. Guignard, Bram Stoker Award® and Shirley Jackson Award winner, author of *A Graveside Gallery***

"In *Penfold's Menu of Magic and Malice*, Valerie B. Williams serves up a full meal of speculative fiction: cursed mirrors that offer glimpses of lost loved ones, fungi that discover the boys hunting them, mermaids hidden in barrels of salt pork, and gnomes with an appetite for more than grave goods. With Penfold himself as a sly, unsettling host, these stories had me lingering over this literary feast. Perfect for readers who savor speculative tales spiced with folklore, gothic dread, and a wicked grin. I loved every word." - **Angela Yuriko Smith, Two-time Bram Stoker Award® winner, publisher of *Space and Time* magazine**

"Valerie Williams hands readers an enticing eight course meal of exquisite tales in *Penfold's Menu of Magic and Malice*. Sixteen dark and fantastic stories with a range that spread from the Appetizer (Myths and Legends) and Soup (Cursed Objects) to the main chow of meaty goodness (Creatures Great and Small). Who is Penfold and why is this sumptuous platter of sixteen stories worth carving up, slowly to enjoy the author's fine grasp of the fantastic that simmers in the shadows? Grab your fork and knife to read about this titular character and the effect he has on this wonderful collection. Williams, like Penfold, has magic up her sleeves in the best, and darkest, ways. Sit down and crack this one open—and bring your appetite. Recommended reading. - **David Simms, Cemetery Dance and author of *Fear The Reaper***

"Replete with monsters, goddesses, cursed objects, and one very hungry giant boar, Valerie B. Williams' *Penfold's Menu of Magic and Malice* is an otherworldly delight! This is a feast that has something that will please every horror reader." - **Douglas Ford, author of *Let's Cut Up Dad! and Other Stories of Transgressive Madness***

"With this collection of delectable dark delights, Valerie B. Williams proves herself to be horror fiction's equivalent of a culinary virtuoso, and these wonderful stories will make a rich banquet for readers!" - **Tim Waggoner, Four-Time Bram Stoker Award® winner and author of *The World Turns Red***

PENFOLD'S MENU OF MAGIC AND MALICE

A COLLECTION OF DARK TALES

VALERIE B. WILLIAMS

PENNY BOOKS PUBLISHING

ISBN: 979-8-9994437-2-4 (paperback)

ISBN: 979-8-9994437-1-7 (ebook)

Cover Art by Ruth Anna Evans, www.ruthannaevans.com

Published by Penny Books Publishing, www.pennybookspublishing.com

PUBLICATION HISTORY

CONTENTS

Introduction	1
APPETIZER - Myths & Legends	3
1. Inheritance	4
2. Hecate's Promise	8
SOUP COURSE - Cursed Objects	26
3. A Delicate Matter	27
4. The Tinker's Gift	39
SALAD COURSE - Plants & Fungi	54
5. Oyster Hunt	55
6. Family Tree	63
PALATE CLEANSER - Evil Children	84
7. Amazing Patsy	85

8. An Echo of Murder   96

FISH COURSE - Mermaids & Pirates   109

9. Salt Pork   110

10. Silent Maidens   122

MEAT COURSE - Creatures Great & Small   131

11. The Wages of Sin   132

12. A Mischief in Gordonsville   139

CHEESE COURSE - Wee Folk   156

13. The Succession   157

14. Shiny Objects   173

DESSERT - The After Times   190

15. Wheels Against Wings   191

16. The Lookout   201

Story Notes   213

Content Warnings   219

Acknowledgements   220

About the Author   222

INTRODUCTION

Greetings! Welcome to this delectable collection of tasty tales. I'm your host and guide, Bartley Penfold—jack of all trades, master of many. You will find out more about me during the soup course.

This is a full menu, comprising eight succulent and satisfying courses, accompanied by wine recommendations. Each course on the menu contains a pair of carefully curated stories. For a taste of what literary pleasures await, please enjoy this amuse-bouche.

· A mysterious visitor to a Civil War hospital offers comfort to the wounded by offering a glimpse of their families if they will only look into his camp mirror.

· Two boys foraging for wild mushrooms discover a new species of fungus at the same time it discovers them.

·   A woman introduces her granddaughter to the matriarchal skill—the ability to charm a carnivorous swamp cryptid.

·   A pirate ship's bounty includes a hogshead containing the body of a young woman, and rumors fly that she is a mermaid.

·   A grave-robbing gnome and his family meet a rookie detective determined to solve the crime and make his name.

·   In a post-apocalyptic world, a father battles his estranged daughter for command of their tribe.

I advise you to pace yourself, both to fully enjoy each course and to prevent over imbibing.

Ah, I hear the dinner bell. You may proceed to the dining room. Bon Appétit!

APPETIZER - Myths & Legends

Recommended Wine: Asti Spumante

INHERITANCE

I pull the phone from my pocket and poke the speed dial with a shaky finger. She picks up on the first ring.

"Auntie, come quickly! Something terrible has happened." I grip the phone in both hands.

"Where are you?"

"The cliffside. We were parking and, and..."

"I'll be right there. Lock the doors and wait."

I throw the phone down and press against the car door. Stan's legs take up most of the floorboard, so I clutch my knees to my chest. I ask myself how this happened. He stares at me with a horrified expression, his outstretched hand forever frozen.

Tonight had been our first real date. I'd been careful all through dinner and at the movie. I had lots of practice—I'd always listened to Auntie. Never look them in the eye, she'd said. She showed me tricks where I would appear to look at a boy, but actually focus on his forehead, ear or chin. Girls...girls were safe. But boys were a dangerous mystery. And since I'd gotten my period, they fascinated me endlessly.

Stan had been such a gentleman all evening, only resting his arm across my shoulders in the theater. When we got to the cliffside, he found a secluded place to park, and we moved to the backseat. I told him I wanted to take it slowly and he listened, for a while. We kissed and he ran his fingers through my coiled locs, telling me how beautiful I was. But when he stroked my breast with his free hand, everything went wrong. I heard a hiss, and he cried out, pulling his hand from my hair.

"What the fuck, Maddy?' He sucked the blood from a wound on his finger.

"Oh, must have been a hairpin," I said, settling my writhing locs with one hand. "Sorry."

He shook the injured hand, then smiled and reached for me. "I'll stick to the soft parts, then."

I fell back into his arms. The heat between us rose and he again reached for my breast with one hand, this time cupping my butt with the other. Heaven! I slid my hands down the back of his jeans and pulled him closer. But something rock hard pressed against me and I panicked. I hadn't looked him in the eyes, had I? I pulled away with a gasp and covered my face.

"No! I'm sorry, Stan. I didn't mean it."

He pulled my hands from my face, and I saw that he was fine! I hadn't hurt him.

"Didn't mean what, Maddy? Talk to me."

He tilted my chin. Relief made me lose my focus and I looked into his eyes. His expression changed and he fell back on the seat, arm still extended.

I stare at his unmoving form, free now to gaze into his beautiful blue eyes, surrounded by a sea of granite gray. What have I done?

A knock comes on the door behind me, and I twist around, muffling a scream. Auntie's face appears in the window. I unlock the door and fall into her arms.

"Ssshh," she says, stroking my locs. They caress her fingers in a show of recognition. "You made a mistake. Now you'll learn how to clean up after yourself."

Together, we maneuver Stan out of the backseat and toward the edge of the cliff. She fetches a sledgehammer from her car, and we get to work. Pieces of stone bounce down the craggy drop. More bits chip off with each impact until the rubble at the bottom of the cliff is unrecognizable as a human shape.

Tears stream down my cheeks as we work. I keep pausing to wipe my runny nose on my sleeve. When the job is done, Auntie wraps her arm around my shoulders and leads me back to her car.

"There, there, Madeline. This time, you didn't mean it. You must forgive yourself. Next time, you'll do it with intent."

"There won't be a next time."

I grow cold as a horrible thought slithers into my mind. I stop at the car door and scrutinize my beloved Auntie's face, so much like my own. The night wind lifts her locs into a halo.

"Auntie, what happened to Uncle Paul?"

HECATE'S PROMISE

Moonlight streams through the bars of the small window in the corner of my cell, bleaching the filth from the straw bedding. I walk to the window and lift my face toward her—a full moon. Similar beams had shone through the window of my cottage twenty-five years ago when, desperate to avoid a terrible future, I'd called upon her Goddess for help. Hecate had heard my plea and granted my wish, for which I had paid dearly. Tomorrow, I will make my final payment.

The old ways became new again in the aftermath of the great wars. Scattered survivors of world-wide battles retreated into small villages and tribes to rebuild life on the blasted earth. As part of this rebirth, the people reacquainted themselves with the deities of their ancestors. Some books remained, but much of the lore about gods and goddesses was handed down by storytellers.

I was only eighteen when I tried to summon the Moon Goddess. I built an altar and adorned it with offerings—white candles, a bowl of salt, a bowl of water, crystals, flowers, a handful of flax, a chalice of wine, a small cauldron, and a bell. The work tired me, and I pressed my hand into the small of my back with a soft moan. My unborn child danced within.

"Patience, little one," I said, stroking my distended belly. "You will be here soon enough."

My child would be named Lucas, after his heroic father. The father who sacrificed his life for a family he didn't know he had. He'd been killed in only his second battle after joining the forces defending our village. His body was buried in the field of battle. Without proof of his death, I imagined it all a terrible mistake until his fellow soldiers told me how he fought and fell. Instead of a funeral, we held a memorial service.

I stifled a sob and continued my preparations, lighting first the candles, then a stick of sage. I waved the smoking herb over the altar.

One week after the memorial service, morning nausea revealed that a part of Lucas lived on inside me. Sophia, the village seer, foretold a son but also warned he would die before his first birthday. How this would happen, she did not say. Determined not to lose both my lover and our son in such a short time, I spent the next few months racing to gather enough knowledge to perform the ceremony before his birth.

The moon, waxing gibbous, poured light through the window. A full moon would better serve the ritual, but my body was waxing at the same pace. My child would arrive before the moon was full.

A damp nose nudged my hand.

"Hello, my sweet," I said, stroking Maya's soft head. Her large brown eyes met mine. My best friend and companion, a sleek black dog with a white diamond on her chest. I'd have not survived the months after losing Lucas but for Maya's constant presence.

"Lay down," I said, motioning to her bed in the corner. She obeyed, but never took her eyes from me.

I dropped the smoking sage into the cauldron and reached for the bell, ringing it three times. I closed my eyes and chanted, "Hecate, Hecate, Hecate." A breeze caressed my face as if something had passed by.

"I am here."

I opened my eyes. On the other side of the altar stood a young woman draped in white robes with gold trim. A colorful floral crown adorned her dark hair. Flanking her were the faint images of two identical women, like reflections. I blinked, but all three forms remained.

"Thank you for coming," I said, scarcely able to believe the ritual had worked. "I need your help." My hand dropped to my belly. "*We* need your help."

Hecate tossed her head and crossed her arms. "Well, what is it you want?" She tapped her sandal-clad foot. "Speak up, girl."

I hadn't known what to expect, but it certainly wasn't a bad-tempered, impatient goddess. Or goddesses, I thought, looking at the three figures.

"My son," I said. "The seer has foretold his death before his first birthday. I wish you to make him strong; strong enough to survive and defeat whatever challenges he faces."

"You wish to change what is preordained?" She raised an eyebrow. "There will be consequences. One change will affect other fates, not always for the best. Are you sure you wish to proceed?"

"Yes!" I nearly shouted the word, so certain was I.

"What will you give me in return?" A cold smile spread across all three faces. She caught sight of Maya, lying quietly in the corner. "This is a lovely dog." She made a kissing noise. To my surprise, Maya rose and went to her.

"Maya! Come here," I called.

My loyal companion ignored me, her adoring gaze fixed on Hecate, her tail drawing slow circles in the air. I swallowed hard, feeling sick.

"She seems to like you," I said faintly.

"Yes." Hecate stroked the dog's head. "She'll do."

"No! You can't have her." The thought of losing my best friend sent shivers through my body.

"Suit yourself."

The baby kicked. Hard. Reminding me of why I'd summoned the Goddess.

"Wait!" I dropped awkwardly to my knees. "At least let me say goodbye to her."

Hecate signaled to Maya, sending her back to me. I held her silken head in my hands and kissed her long snout. I threw my arms around her. She accepted the hug stiffly, then trotted back to her new mistress. The dog I adored was already gone. I peered through a veil of tears at the cold-hearted Goddess.

"Will you grant my wish? Make my son strong?"

"I promise," said Hecate.

I dropped my head into my hands and wept. When I lifted my eyes, Hecate and my beloved Maya were gone.

My son was born two days later, a tiny and sickly baby. I feared I had surrendered Maya in vain. Lucas rallied slowly, gaining weight and becoming stronger. On his second birthday, I began to relax and believe that Hecate had kept her promise. But I couldn't help but wonder if Lucas' progress wasn't due, at least in part, to my own efforts.

Annabelle, the village healer, had attended Lucas' birth. She continued to care for us in the early days afterward, and we became close. She brought me potions and tonics to build his strength on her frequent visits. Annabelle was such a constant presence in our home that Lucas began to call her "Auntie."

When Lucas started school at age five, he wasn't the tallest or strongest boy in his class, but he was healthy. He had his father's gift of charm—the other children idolized him, and soon he had a retinue of small followers. My kitchen was filled with children's laughter. Our small family grew when Annabelle gave me a puppy from her dog's latest litter, a fluffy brown bitch I named Iris. The puppy immediately attached herself to Lucas. I was fond of Iris but, after the loss of Maya, was unwilling to open my heart to another dog.

I had no desire to remarry. After the loss of my true love, what would be the point? My family was complete with a healthy son, good friends, and a good life.

When Lucas was thirteen, a knock on the door one afternoon interrupted my dinner preparations. The schoolmaster stood on my doorstep with a firm grasp on my son's arm. Lucas stared at his feet.

"Master Angelos. Lucas," I said in surprise.

The schoolmaster frowned. "There's been an incident."

I looked at Lucas, who still refused to meet my eyes.

"Come in." I stepped back and led them to the living room.

"Adrian was badly beaten this afternoon," the schoolmaster began, after refusing my offer of tea. "Your son and three other boys are responsible."

"Lucas? Is this true?"

"Adrian had been spreading tales about me." Lucas said, his face expressionless. He looked small, as though he had shrunk into himself.

"Another child saw what happened," said Master Angelos. "The boys cornered Adrian. They held him while Lucas delivered the first blows. When he was done, the others did the same." He shook his head. "It became a competition to see which boy could inflict the most damage. Adrian is with the healer as we speak."

I glared at my son. "Go to your room. I'll deal with you later."

Lucas slunk away, scuffing his feet. I walked the schoolmaster to the door.

"Thank you for bringing him home. I'm sorry he was involved in this. That's not the way I raised him."

Master Angelos gave me a searching look. "Your son is very charismatic. It appears the attack was his idea, and his friends followed."

"He can't control the other boys!" I blurted.

"He had me fooled for some time." The man placed a hand on my shoulder. "Don't underestimate how strong his influence can be."

"Lucas will be punished, I promise you. And I'll keep a close eye on him, you can be sure."

I marched to Lucas' room and flung open the door. He sat on his bed, staring out the window. He turned his head and smiled without a trace of shame.

"What do you have to say for yourself?" I asked, sitting next to him.

"I encouraged Adrian to stop spreading tales."

"Encouraged? Couldn't you have talked it out? Told a teacher? Told me?"

Lucas took my hand. "I didn't want to worry you, Mother. I wanted to handle this on my own." He kissed my cheek.

I pulled him to me and stroked his hair. "You know I love you, but I'm very disappointed."

He burst into tears. If I'd struck him, he could not have been more shattered. I soothed him until the sobs died down, then pulled away. I held his face in my hands.

"You must apologize to Adrian. And I will walk you to and from school for now."

"Mother!"

I held up a finger. "No argument. You've broken my trust and must earn it back."

The next day, I called on Annabelle. She had patched up Adrian and sent him home but was still shaken by the extent of his injuries.

"I can't believe young boys to be capable of such violence, especially not Lucas!" she said.

"I'm shocked as well. But I believe Lucas is truly sorry. I'll be keeping him on a very short leash for a while."

Annabelle clasped my hand. "If there's anything I can do..."

I hugged her and went home.

But before I could walk Lucas to school even once, Master Angelos declared that Lucas would not be allowed to return. Adrian's parents insisted. My appeal fell on deaf ears, and my son's formal education ended.

Lucas continued to read the few books I owned. I gave him lessons during the time I wasn't sewing and repairing clothing for the villagers, our sole means of support. I encouraged him to look for work so as not to get bored. The trouble he might get into was an unspoken concern. He was always good with his hands and began an apprenticeship with the village blacksmith.

Despite my son's continued good behavior, a seed of doubt had been planted. During long hours of repetitive work, I recalled incidents from his early childhood that I had dismissed. When Lucas was about eight, Annabelle's prized amulet went missing after he had spent the day with her. When I found it later in his room, he said he must have accidentally bundled it up with his belongings when he left her house. Both Annabelle and I believed him. But now I wondered.

More worrisome was the fate of Iris. The little dog followed him everywhere, accompanying him to school and waiting patiently outside to walk him home. About a year after the amulet incident, Iris disappeared. We searched frantically for her, enlisting the aid of neighbors. By the time her remains were found deep in the woods, scavengers had done their work. Only scraps of her fluffy brown fur remained to identify her. Lucas was inconsolable. For a day. Then he moved on as if he'd never had a dog. When I asked if he wanted another, he said a dog would just get in his way.

Had Iris gotten in his way?

Lucas had been at the forge for six months when I made my decision. I waited until he left for work before gathering offerings for Hecate. I spread them on the altar, lit the sage, rang the bell, and chanted her name. Nothing happened. I rang the bell again, chanted again. On the third try the Goddess appeared with her two shadows, looking annoyed.

"I am here. What do you want?"

"Thank you, Goddess. I am worried about my son."

"Is he not alive and thriving? Is he not strong, as promised?"

"Yes, Goddess. He is. But he is also cruel and manipulative."

She waved her hand as if swatting a fly. "And? You asked for strength. The other qualities work hand-in-hand with strength to ensure your son's survival. Would you put his life at risk by having me remove them?"

"No, of course not," I said, terrified at the thought of losing him. "Can you make him only cruel when necessary?"

Hecate laughed. "He decides what is necessary. You're his mother. Now that you are aware of all the facets of his nature, you can influence him as you see fit."

My shoulders slumped and I shook my head. "Lucas is a strong-willed young man."

Hecate's faces softened. The three figures whispered together and came to a decision.

"Wait until the new moon and go to the crossroads. I have a gift to ease your burden."

"I will," I said eagerly. "But what...?"

Hecate blinked out as if she was never there.

On the eve of the new moon, I listened to my son snoring. The potion I'd slipped into his drink at dinner would keep him in a deep sleep until morning. Lifting my cloak from the hook, I slipped out the door.

I stood in the center of the dark crossroads and waited. A rustle sounded from the woods and Hecate stepped out, accompanied by a familiar shape.

"Maya!" I ran toward my beloved dog. Unlike me, she hadn't aged in the years since the goddess took her. Maya whimpered and licked my face, wagging her tail furiously. I looked through tear-filled eyes at Hecate. "You've taken good care of her."

"Of course. And now I am returning her to you. May you find strength in her presence. You are no longer alone."

"Thank you, Goddess!"

"This dog," she pointed, "is the only reason I have humored your impertinence. You have your son and your dog. Make the best of it." With a swish of her robes, she disappeared into the woods from whence she came.

Lucas had heard me speak of Maya many times. When he awoke to our new family member, he saw the resemblance.

"She'll be good company for you I imagine," he said, giving the dog a perfunctory pat on the head. "Don't you want to give her a different name?"

"She looks so like my old dog it's as if she's been returned to me," I said. "Maya is a perfect name."

After that introduction, Lucas paid little attention to her. But any time he was at home, Maya watched him. When he hugged me, she pressed against my side. Once, when he was relating a conversation with a customer at the forge, he waved his hands close to my face. Maya gave a low growl and bared her teeth.

"Maya! He wasn't hurting me," I said, smoothing her hackles.

Lucas laughed. "You don't want to start something you can't finish," he said to the dog.

I frowned.

Lucas saw my expression and added, "Joking, Mother."

Was he? I questioned even the most innocuous actions of my son, always on the alert for cruelty and vindictiveness. My vigilance continued as Lucas grew into a young man, and I believe I averted many situations fraught with the potential for violence. But I could not be with him all the time.

As Lucas entered his twenties, he developed an interest in politics. At twenty-one, he was elected mayor of our small village of Pefka by a landslide. Unsurprisingly, he had a loyal staff to act as his eyes and ears. Any problems in Pefka were quickly identified and solved—the bridge repaired, another healer brought to the village, and taxes lowered.

When the magistrate governing the borough containing Pefka (one of over thirty other villages) died, Lucas ran for the position. Despite his youth, his success as mayor, his loyal supporters, and his personal charm won him the position. Along with the title came a grand house in the capital city of Tavros. While proud of his accomplishments, I worried about him being so far from my steadying hand. But he was a grown man and a successful politician.

The position of magistrate came with great power. Lucas reveled in having citizens obey his commands, no matter how petty or senseless. He amused himself by pitting men against each other in battles to the death, at first using slaves, but then anyone who angered him. An attractive woman could be summoned to his bedchamber, regardless of marital status. Rumors flew that it became a point of pride among his sycophants to have one's wife chosen by the magistrate. Women who refused were never seen again.

Discontent spread throughout the borough. An opposition group formed quietly, wary of the consequences of angering the somehow still popular magistrate. My friend Annabelle led the opposition party in Pefka. While I couldn't publicly join the group, I secretly supported the cause with the money Lucas sent me to show his subjects what a good son he was.

As the time for elections approached, Lucas had a competitor for the position, and professed his belief in fair elections as part of democracy. Just before the election, the other candidate was "accidentally" killed by a runaway horse and cart, leaving Lucas still in power and his opposition cowed. The day after the election celebrations, Lucas had Annabelle arrested and thrown into prison. I traveled to Tavros to meet with my son.

I'd seen the private areas of the magistrate's mansion on prior visits, but this time I was escorted to the grand hall. Cold marble walls surrounded an open area facing a dais holding a long table in front of a row of chairs. Lucas sat in the middle, conferring with his lieutenants, He looked up.

"Mother! How lovely to see you."

He crossed the large room and kissed me on the cheek, then stroked Maya. Maya's lip curled ever so slightly.

I knew it was all for show. His loyal staff, ever present, watched our every move.

"May we speak privately?" I asked.

"Of course."

He led me to a small antechamber and called for a jug of wine and two cups. When the servant had departed, he turned to me with his most charming smile.

"Your Auntie Annabelle! How could you?" I blurted. My determination to stay calm was swept away by the sight of his smug face.

"Now Mother," he said in a soothing voice, "a ruler can't tolerate rebellion. It makes him look weak." He shook his head. "I hated to do it, but I had no choice."

"Of course you had a choice! Annabelle was like a second mother to you. You may as well have arrested me."

The calculating look he gave me chilled me to the bone.

"She will have a fair trial. And if she is found not guilty of treason, she will be released," he said, taking a sip of wine.

"And if she's found guilty?"

He stared at me, stone-faced.

—◦✦◦—

I returned to Pefka and contacted the disheartened members of the opposition. At a meeting in my home, I convinced them that we could still stop Lucas. Annabelle's arrest, and my status as the mother of the tyrant, convinced them that the only way to be rid of Lucas was a coup. The election had failed, and Lucas would only become more dangerous. If he died in the coup, so be it.

News traveled slowly, so by the time word reached us of Annabelle's "trial," she'd been found guilty and hanged as a traitor. I felt sick. I had interfered with the seer's prediction out of fear of losing my son. My selfishness had cost a good woman her life, and she was only one of many. We sped up our plans.

Lucas was due to visit Pefka the following week. He and his men were to be feted at a celebratory feast. I had used Annabelle's formula to concoct a sleeping draught for the wine. When his guard was down, our volunteers would strike.

I waited in the square to greet him before his address to his old friends and neighbors. He dismounted his horse and handed the reins to the valet. He stepped forward and embraced me.

"How could you do this, Mother?" he hissed in my ear as he pinned my arms to my sides.

His guards surrounded us and marched me to the village jail, where I sit tonight with Maya by my side.

⸻◈⸻

I don't expect to sleep on this, my last night on earth. The hangman's noose awaits me in the morning, upon the order of my own flesh and blood. I have nothing left to lose. Without benefit of altar or offerings, I try to summon the Moon Goddess. I squeeze my eyes shut and pray to her on my knees, begging her indulgence one last time. When I feel her presence, relief steals the strength from my body. I collapse and gaze up at her glowing tripartite form.

"Hecate! You came."

"Your son outmaneuvered you. I'm disappointed." Her voice is soft, almost sad.

"As am I."

"I warned you. One never knows what ripples a change to the future will set off."

Hecate calls Maya. The dog glances at me as if to apologize, then obeys.

"You know he'll kill her, don't you," she says, stroking the dog's head.

"Yes." Wrenching sobs shake me. I recover my breath enough to ask one last favor. "Goddess, I've earned my death, but Maya is innocent. Will you care for her?"

Hecate doesn't reply, looking at me thoughtfully. She continues to stroke the dog.

"That is the first unselfish request you've made. Of course I will take her. And I grant you peace for the rest of your life, however short it may be."

The goddess and my beloved dog disappear for the last time. Calmness and serenity settle over me like a soft blan-

ket. As Hecate promised, I am at peace. I pray for Lucas'
future victims—may he meet justice someday.

Dawn breaks through the barred window. I hear heavy
footsteps and the clank of armor.

My dear friend Annabelle awaits.

SOUP COURSE - CURSED OBJECTS

Recommended Wine: Pinot Noir

A DELICATE MATTER

London, November 5, 1887

Dr. Dinwiddie hurried toward the Bethnal Green Home for Mothers and Babies. Likely too late for the delivery, he might be able to render some assistance to the mother. A grim scene awaited.

The midwife was screaming and holding a limp blue baby in her arms. The child's eyes bulged and its swollen, purple tongue protruded from its mouth. The mother, who should have been exhausted, struggled to snatch the child. Her fingers clawed the unfortunate midwife down the left side of her face. The stout woman resisted and turned away, still trying to protect the baby. Dr. Dinwiddie grabbed the mother's arm. She turned, her face red, her mouth twisted into a soundless snarl, and lunged toward the doctor. He pinned her arms to her sides. She fought with the strength of one possessed.

"What the devil is going on here?" he shouted. "Belladonna, Mrs. Avery! In my satchel!"

The midwife placed the infant in a cot, grabbed the brown glass bottle, and forced its thick liquid contents down the hysterical woman's throat.

After a few minutes, the new mother slumped back into the bed.

"I only left for a minute to get more towels, doctor," the midwife wailed, a hand pressed to her bloody cheek. "When I come back, she's strangling the babe!" She poked the small, silent body in the cot. "I think he's dead."

Dinwiddie nodded and turned to look at the unconscious mother.

"Was the delivery normal?"

"Normal in every way, doctor. She were very brave." Mrs. Avery shook her head. "Then she went mad."

Dinwiddie had been responsible for placing Miss Hobbes in the Home. Lord Bromley, her prior employer, had been livid when her gravid state had begun to show. He'd contacted Dinwiddie as one known for being able to help gentlemen in certain situations.

Dinwiddie's eyes fell to Miss Hobbes' right hand, where she wore a small ring with turquoise stones and seed pearls surrounding a square-cut, deep red garnet. He had given her the ring when he left her at the Home, telling her it was a gift from Lord Bromley. The band of the ring formed two hands, one holding each side of the setting.

"Like his Lordship holding me in his hands every day," the former maid had exclaimed, face flushed with pleasure. "I shall never take it off!"

The midwife cleared her throat, bringing him back to the present and his responsibilities.

"Mrs. Avery, the child was stillborn." The doctor spoke with the authority of his station.

"But doctor..." The midwife wrinkled her brow.

"Do you understand?" He pressed two shillings into her palm.

Her face cleared. "Yes, doctor. Of course. I'll help the vicar prepare the poor mite for burial." She scooped up the small body and left the room.

Miss Hobbes moaned and began to thrash. Her sweat-soaked hair was plastered to her head, the bottom of her gown bloodstained. Dinwiddie quickly pulled a set of leather straps from his satchel and bound her wrists and ankles to the bed. She opened her eyes, lifted her head and looked wildly around the room.

"Where is my son? His Lordship must see our son!"

The doctor leaned over and looked at the woman's face. Her teeth snapped at the air and he pulled back. No trace of sanity remained in her eyes. He placed his hand over her cuffed right wrist.

"There, there. Mrs. Avery is just cleaning him up and will bring him back shortly. You must rest now."

She settled her head on the pillow with a sigh. Gradually her breathing slowed, and she closed her eyes. Once she was snoring softly, Dinwiddie slid the ring off her hand, pocketed it, and left the room, locking the door on his way out.

He paused at Matron's office before leaving. "Miss Hobbes has contracted acute melancholia as a result of the stillbirth. Please contact Dr. Thwaite at the Mercy Lunatic Asylum to have her moved." He pushed a £5 note into her hand and stepped into the chilly London drizzle before she could question him.

Lord Bromley had been angry when it appeared that Miss Hobbes would carry to term. "You told me I wouldn't have to worry about the child," he said.

"You won't," assured the doctor, hiding his own concern.

Lord Bromley would not have to worry now about a bastard soiling his good name. And Miss Hobbes, even if she recovered her senses, would already be in the madhouse. Memories of her hands around the baby's neck might return, but if she confessed, no one would believe her.

Dinwiddie swayed with the motion of the carriage taking him away from the Bethnal Green Home, fondling the ring in his pocket, remembering when he had first seen it. Three years earlier, he'd stopped at the Lamb and Flag for a much-needed pint. A darkly tanned, khaki-clad soldier with sergeant's insignia had stepped up to the bar and fumbled in his pockets for money.

"Allow me," said Dinwiddie, placing a coin on the bar.

"Thank ye, sir," said the soldier. The man's face was drawn and his eyes unfocused.

"Served in India?" asked Dinwiddie.

The soldier's face twisted in pain, then he forced a weak smile. "Yes, sir. May I never see that cursed land again. All that was good in my life remains buried in its soil." He took a deep draught of ale and wiped his mouth, staring straight ahead, then continued as if speaking to himself.

"My wife, my beautiful Evangeline, and my unborn daughter. She would have been named Miriam, after my mother." Tears ran down his face unchecked.

"The doctors couldn't save them?"

"Hah! They never got a chance. Evangeline took a knife to her belly and cut the child out. She left the babe pinned to our bed like a butterfly and leapt from the balcony. The heat! It was the heat drove her mad." He dropped his head into his hands and wept.

Dinwiddie patted the man awkwardly on the back. "There, there, old chap."

The soldier stood abruptly. "I must go. Thank you for your kindness." He reached into his pocket. "I don't want to remember them anymore." He placed a woman's garnet and turquoise ring on the bar and stumbled away.

Dinwiddie examined the ring. It was exquisite. He picked it up, put it in his pocket, and finished his pint.

When Dinwiddie arrived home that evening, he presented it to Emma, his bride of one year.

"Robert," she exclaimed, turning her hand from side to side, "it's beautiful. Thank you so, so much."

She threw her arms around him and kissed him passionately, heedless of the chambermaid stoking the fire in the parlor. He flushed and took her hands in his, moving away from her as he did so. Emma was 15 years his junior, full of youthful exuberance and scorn for tradition.

While her unconventional ways sometimes embarrassed him, he wasn't bothered that night when she came to his bedchamber. Normally shy and reticent about lovemaking, she surprised him by slipping out of her dressing gown and into his bed. That night, she was transformed from an inexperienced young wife into a confident paramour.

The following months were the happiest of his life. Emma's confidence and hunger for him in the marriage bed continued. She initiated lovemaking two or three times a week, even when he came home late from surgery. The frequency only slowed as her pregnancy advanced.

Emma had confided in him during those joyous moments that she was certain she'd become pregnant the night he'd brought home the ring. They had been trying to conceive ever since they were married. She swore the ring was a good luck charm and never removed it.

Dinwiddie had been at a medical convention in York when Emma miscarried. By the time word got to him to return home at once, she had died, along with their tiny son.

At the funeral parlor, he kissed her cold lips and reached for her hand. The deep red garnet glinted from the ring on her finger, mocking him. Furious, he worked the ring off and thrust it into his pocket, fully intending to throw the cursed object into the Thames.

After the funeral, Dinwiddie moved through his routines like a sleepwalker. In losing Emma, he'd lost his joy. He didn't save one thought for the unnamed baby, at least partially blaming the child for his beautiful young wife's death. The ring remained in the deep pocket of the coat he'd worn the day of the funeral until the day Lord Evanston's man showed up.

Late for his first appointment, Dinwiddie had opened the door to find a liveried footman on the front step, requesting his presence at Lord Evanston's estate to discuss a "delicate matter." Dinwiddie had only met Evanston once, at a charity ball to benefit the local hospital, where his Lordship had made a rather large donation.

After a swift carriage ride, a butler ushered him into the parlor, where Evanston stood with his hands behind his back gazing out the tall windows into the garden. The butler withdrew, closing the door firmly.

"Woodley tells me you were very helpful to him last year," Evanston began without turning.

"Mr. Woodley was concerned about Miss...."

"I know what he was concerned about." Evanston paced in front of the window. "My chambermaid, Miss O'Neil, has gotten herself in the family way. She can't work and she can't stay here."

Evanston spun about, meeting Dinwiddie's eyes for the first time.

"The stupid girl also seems to think I'm the baby's father. Ridiculous, of course." He pulled out a mono-grammed handkerchief, blew his nose, and stuffed the silk cloth back in his pocket.

Reflexively, Dinwiddie put his hand in his own pocket and felt the small metal band, forgotten until now.

"Can you take care of this? As you did for Woodley?" Evanston asked brusquely.

"Of course, Your Lordship."

Dinwiddie's services to the gentry had thus far used traditional methods, such as pennyroyal tea and other established means to bring about miscarriages in those unsuspecting patients. After returning from the Evanston estate, he removed the ring from his pocket and laid it on the table. Time had moderated his grief and revived his scientific curiosity. Could the ring serve as an abortifacient?

Upon returning from Evanston's estate, Dinwiddie wrote to his old schoolmate, Brian Godfrey, now a Major with the 63rd Regiment in Peshawar. He'd not gotten the name of the sergeant who had given him the ring, but Brian may be able to help. The bizarre nature of the soldier's tale should jar his friend's memory, if he had indeed heard of it. He posted the letter the next morning.

In the meantime, he moved ahead with his service to Lord Evanston and escorted Molly O'Neil to the Sacred Heart Home (as she was Catholic). He'd already tried the standard solutions, to no avail. Miss O'Neil was as healthy as a brood mare and seemed likely to carry her bastard to term. In desperation, he presented her the ring. Another miscarriage, another sad maternal death.

His suspicions had been correct, and he'd had no reason to believe the ring would affect Miss Hobbes any differently than it had his beloved Emma or Miss O'Neil. Hobbes' rapid descent into madness had surprised and frightened him. It was more like what happened to the soldier's wife, Evangeline. Miscarriage and death in childbirth was an entirely unremarkable event. Murder and madness, however, would draw unwelcome attention.

A thick envelope postmarked Peshawar, India, lay on his desk when he arrived home after dealing with Miss Hobbes. With shaking hands, he tore it open and began to read.

Dear Robert,

I hope this letter finds you well. My belated condolences on the loss of your wife.

I am familiar with the tale you heard. Sergeant Bridges deserted over three years ago. His body was found hanging near the docks in London. He appeared to have taken his own life.

The facts of his story are true. Mrs. Bridges was found dead at the foot of her balcony with deep slashes in her abdomen and an empty womb. The child was found on the bed as described. No one else was home, and Sergeant Bridges said he discovered the bodies. When questioned, he blamed first the heat, then the ring for driving his wife mad.

He said he acquired the ring from an old sadhu after his death. The man's daughter claimed Bridges stole it, but he said the man had promised it to him. When he refused to return it, the daughter cursed him and whomever the ring should pass to. We were unable to locate the woman, so have only Bridges' word about these events. We issued a warrant for Sergeant Bridges' arrest for the murder of his wife and child, but he had fled the country.

I firmly believe Bridges was delusional, and that his wife and child died at his hands. Nevertheless, I have seen many things in this strange country that defy reason and logic, so I remain cautious. You should also exercise caution when considering what you wish to do with that ring. It has a black history.

Yours,

Brian

Dinwiddie folded the letter, returned it to the envelope, and shuffled to his bedroom. He placed the ring on the bureau before getting into bed. The evening's events had shaken him, and he was tired to his core. The doctor dreamed of tiny bodies born too soon, blue babies, babies with knives driven through them.

A heavy panting sound woke him. He opened his eyes to a dark figure looming over the bed.

"Don't move," said a female voice.

He ignored the command and rose, only to be slashed across the arm. The moonlight showed Miss Hobbes, eyes no longer wild but fixed on him in a steady, cool gaze. In her right hand she held a scalpel, dark with his blood.

"What did you do to me to make me murder my own child?"

"Miss Hobbes, you're not well. Let me take you back to the hospital," begged Dinwiddie, pressing his left hand over his arm, trying to stop the flow of blood.

She slashed again, this time opening a gash across his chest. "You mean the loony bin! No, doctor. I'll not go."

The madwoman gave a sly smile and shifted the scalpel to her left hand, holding up her right so that he could see the ring, now slick with his own blood. "Did you want this so badly you would poison me to get it?"

"Take it off!" he cried.

The scalpel rose and fell over and over.

—·◈·—

Screams and moans echoed in the dank hallways of the Mercy Lunatic Asylum, but the newly returned occupant of cell G lay silent and still. Washed of blood and clad in a fresh gown, she slumbered in an opium-induced haze. The floor nurse locked the door to the cell and returned the keys to her belt, the moonlight catching a crimson flash from her right hand.

The Tinker's Gift

Corporal Clarence Hutchinson remembered well the day Bartley Penfold arrived at Abrams House with a clatter and a song. His canvas-sided wagon bore the words "Penfold's Knife Sharpening & Other Repairs." Hidden metal objects clanged against each other in rhythm with the plodding steps of the large black dray horse. Penfold sang a hymn in a strong tenor voice as the wagon approached the wide front porch. He doffed his bowler hat at Mrs. Forsythe as he sang the final refrain, "bringing in the sheaves."

"Good afternoon, Madam." His gaze ran across the line of wounded soldiers in gray—sitting, standing, and leaning in front of the large house. "May I offer my services? I can sharpen surgical instruments, repair pots and pans, or work metal into any tool you need."

Penfold looked directly at Hutchinson and smiled, showing crooked yellow teeth. Trapped in the gaze of the tinker, Hutchinson felt light-headed. He looked away and immediately felt better. He stared hard at the blanket covering his lap, and what remained of his right leg, and listened as the man continued.

"I also happen to be an ordained minister. I could provide spiritual comfort to these brave men."

Mrs. Forsythe frowned and tapped her forefinger against closed lips before speaking. "All strangers are welcome to a meal and a night of rest at my home. If you can provide the services you state, you may be able to stay longer."

"I will remain as long as I am helpful. I want nothing more than to support our soldiers in any way I can. Sadly, I am too old to don the uniform."

And as simply as that, Penfold was in.

Mrs. Forsythe was the mistress of Abrams House, a stately Virginia mansion which had been converted to a convalescent hospital. Her husband led a regiment currently fighting in Pennsylvania while she supported the cause at home. She was quite discerning, so her easy acceptance of Penfold had surprised Hutchinson. The man seemed a bit "off," but Hutchinson was the only one who noticed.

Penfold wasted no time getting to know everyone in and around Abrams House, from soldiers to slaves. His age showed in his deeply lined face and iron gray hair, but he was as spry as a spring lamb, moving easily around his forge as he repaired and constructed tools and instruments. As meticulous about his appearance as his work, he was never seen without a vest and cravat, hair oiled and slicked back. A small camp mirror dangled from his belt, assuredly for him to check that no hair was out of place.

After a few days of working his trade for the hospital and for Mrs. Forsythe, he began making regular visits to the men on the ward, inquiring if they had any belongings in need of repair, and offering to pray with them if they wished. Most of the soldiers had few if any possessions, so Penfold could often be seen standing with head bowed, murmuring words intended only for the occupant of the cot.

Hutchinson declined all Penfold's offers of prayer, begging off as tired and in need of rest. The part-time preacher took the refusal in stride, with a yellow smile and a "God Bless you, soldier," as he moved on to the next man.

Hutchinson woke from a midday doze to hear Penfold speaking to Private Evans in the adjoining cot. Evans had been feverish and coughing, spending much of his time wheezing in opium-induced sleep. The smell of mustard plasters rose from his overheated body.

"Would you like to see them?" asked Penfold.

"More than anything, sir. My little Charity will be three years old next month. She was hardly walking when last I saw her."

Hutchinson kept his back turned and feigned sleep. He heard a rustling of clothing, followed by a click.

"Oh!" gasped Evans. "Look! It's Eva. And there's sweet Charity. Hello! Hello!"

"They cannot hear you. Or see you. The mirror only allows you to view them, not speak to them."

Evans began to sob. "They look so happy."

"They are, except that they miss you. But they are proud of you. And the Lord will care for them after you are gone."

"Gone? But I'm going to return to them. As soon as I get better!"

"Of course you will all be reunited. In God's time."

Hutchinson heard the stool creak as Penfold stood.

"Get some rest, my son."

The next morning Evans was a new man. Hutchinson awoke to find him perched on the edge of his cot, cheeks ruddy with life. The man even took a brief, although slow, walk around the ward. When Hutchinson touched Evans' shoulder, the heat that had radiated from his body was gone.

"Fever broke. That's what the doctor said. I feel well enough to walk out of here and home to my family."

"I don't think you're ready for that quite yet," said Hutchinson. "But you do look much better." He cleared his throat, then blurted out the question that had been foremost in his mind. "What did you see in Mr. Penfold's mirror?"

Evans' eyes widened and he smiled broadly. "My girls, moving about. Eva was hanging wash on the line while Charity played at her feet. It was like looking into the garden through a windowpane. Magical! You should ask him. I'm sure he'd let you see your family as well."

Hutchinson was not the only person Evans told. By the end of the day, the story of the tinker's magical mirror had spread throughout the ward. But Penfold was nowhere to be found. His wagon and forge still stood where they had for the past few weeks, but the man himself had disappeared.

The next day, Evans was discovered dead in his cot, all signs of his miraculous recovery gone. The body was ashen and shrunken, skin stretched tight as if all its moisture had fled. But the soldier had died with a smile on his face.

Penfold reappeared around mid-morning. He looked refreshed, as if he'd just woken from a long nap. He claimed to have taken a walk in the forest and gotten lost, returning to his wagon in the wee hours. He immediately offered to perform the burial service for the unfortunate Evans. Hutchinson's wheelchair couldn't negotiate the rocky path to the growing cemetery behind the stables, so he heard second-hand about the powerful sermon that brought Mrs. Forsythe to tears.

With Penfold's return, many soldiers began to beg for a glimpse into his mirror. He denied all requests except those of the sickest. Over the course of the next two weeks, three more soldiers had miraculous one-day recoveries, followed by an overnight death. All died smiling.

Rumblings of suspicion began. Soldiers stopped asking to look into Penfold's mirror, terrified that the vision would cost them their lives.

Mrs. Forsythe called Penfold to the library. Raised voices were heard, but eventually the door opened and the two walked out arm in arm. They went directly to the ward, where a slave banged on a bucket until the murmuring ceased and all attention turned to Mrs. Forsythe. Bartley Penfold stood next to her, head down and hands clasped. Hutchinson detected a smirk on the tinker's face—a face noticeably smoother than when he arrived at Abrams House.

"Gentlemen," said Mrs. Forsythe. "It has come to my attention that you believe Mr. Penfold here," she nodded toward him, "is responsible for the deaths of Evans, Sullivan, Murgatroyd, and Fitzpatrick. I don't need to remind you how grievously ill these men were." She scanned the room while soldiers dropped their eyes to avoid her gaze. "This is a hospital. Men die despite our best efforts. Contrary to being responsible for the deaths of these men, Mr. Penfold gave them a great gift." She stopped and stepped back, yielding the stage.

"Brave men," Penfold began. "I am saddened that you would think I meant harm to any one of you. But I understand that what occurred is hard to believe." He reached for the small mirror on his belt. It was an oval, about 6 inches tall and 3 inches wide, framed in wood with a wood cover that swiveled to cover the glass when not in use. He held it up, cover closed. "This mirror is an instrument of God!" His stentorian tone filled the room.

Murmuring began again, until Mrs. Forsythe motioned for quiet.

"This mirror was given to me by a dying soldier. He told me it allowed a glimpse of one's beloved. But only if that person were dying would the mirror work. You see, the mirror doesn't cause death but eases one's passing into the Heavenly Kingdom." Penfold raised his arms and eyes to the sky.

Rather than soothing the men, this revelation sent them into a panic. If Penfold approached them, they refused his visits and avoided eye contact just in case he offered the mirror. No dying man wants to believe he is dying. And the others weren't convinced that the mirror wasn't the cause of rather than the companion to the journey.

Instead of individual visits, Penfold began to lead daily morning prayers for all willing to attend. There was a surprisingly robust turnout. The soldiers wanted to keep a good relationship with God, as long as they weren't on the receiving end of individual attention from His messenger.

Hutchinson was firmly in the camp of those who suspected Penfold's mirror was assisting, if not directly causing, the deaths. An undercurrent of fear joined the feeling of unease he'd always had when in the vicinity of the tinker. Despite the fact that Penfold had never been anything but gracious to him, Hutchinson did not trust the man. He was more determined than ever to get out of the wheelchair and leave Abrams House, and Bartley Penfold, behind forever.

Hutchinson practiced using his crutch, at first by making his way around the ward several times a day. As he gained strength, he added a slow circuit of the grounds, which brought him past the tinker's forge tucked away near the barn. Mornings were ideal for his walks, since Penfold was busy leading prayers and Hutchinson never attended them anyway.

One gray morning after a heavy rain, Hutchinson crutched along the path with eyes downcast, careful to skirt large puddles but unable to avoid the thick mud. He sweated profusely in the cool air, working twice as hard to travel half as far, while the sucking mud yanked at his boot and attempted to wrest the crutch from his grasp. Stopping to catch his breath, he discovered he was right next to Penfold's wagon. The canvas sides were drawn down, as usual, but the back flap was rolled up.

Hutchinson's already rapid pulse increased at the opportunity to find out more about the tinker. He glanced around quickly, then moved closer and peered into the darkness inside. Shelves filled with jars and bundles lined the inside of the structure. His phantom right leg twitched with the desire to be of use, but the crutch was a poor substitute, and he could not climb the three steep steps to enter the wagon for a closer look.

"May I help you?" boomed a familiar voice behind him.

Hutchinson whirled. Or attempted to. The crutch skidded in the mud, and he lost his balance. His head cracked against the top step, and everything went black.

He awoke on a straw mattress, looking at a canvas ceiling. The smells of metal, Macassar oil, and damp assaulted his nostrils and he sneezed. An oil lantern provided dim light. Penfold's face filled his vision as the tinker leaned over him, brow furrowed with concern.

"Ah, there you are. You gave me quite a fright, Corporal."

Panicked at his vulnerable position, Hutchinson pushed up on his elbows, then fell back with a moan as his head exploded with pain.

"Doctor," he gasped.

"I've already sent for the doctor. He said not to move and that he would be here soon." Penfold stepped away. "Would you like something to eat? I'm afraid all I can offer is coffee and hardtack. I could have something brought from the house."

Hutchinson lay still, stomach churning and head pounding. "Not hungry," he said through clenched teeth.

Penfold returned to the bedside. He fondled the mirror hanging from his belt, running his fingers over the smooth wooden cover. Hutchinson quickly clamped his eyes shut.

But rather than proferring the mirror, Penfold began to pray.

"Oh Lord, please heal this brave man, who has fought for you and for his country. Amen."

Too weak to resist years of habit, Hutchinson heard an automatic "Amen" come from his lips. He opened his eyes.

Penfold captured Hutchinson in his dark-eyed gaze. "While we wait for the doctor, I have a story to tell. Would you like to hear it?"

Trapped, Hutchinson willed his tongue to object, but it lay mute in his mouth like a somnolent slug. He tried to move his head only to find that paralyzed as well. What kind of magician was this strange man?

Penfold pulled the mirror from his belt and held it in front of Hutchinson's face, cover closed. With one slight movement of his thumb, he could expose the mirror and send Hutchinson to his death.

"God does not perform His miracles without cost," said the itinerant preacher. "Our faith He expects, but for some things He demands more. The cost for me has been to never stop moving, never have a home, to continually seek out souls to help. I must confess to feeling some envy for the men with families, who can view their loved ones for the final time. I have no one."

He stopped with a sigh, rubbed a hand over his smooth face then ran his fingers through jet-black hair. There had been two more deaths and Penfold now looked twenty years younger than when he had arrived. Even his yellow teeth had whitened.

When Penfold rubbed his face, he broke eye contact and thus released Hutchinson. The soldier rolled his head to the left to avoid being mesmerized again and spotted a row of glass jars on the shelves next to the bed. Penfold droned on, deep in his own world of self-pity. Hutchinson snaked his arm out from under the thin blanket and grabbed a jar, surprised at its weight. It rattled when he lifted it and Penfold turned toward him, but too late. Hutchinson smashed the jar against the side of the tinker's head. Penfold slumped across him with blood running from his temple.

Ignoring his own pounding head, Hutchinson pushed the man onto the floor and grabbed the camp mirror from his hand. He turned the surface away and slid the cover open. When Penfold groaned and awoke, he found himself staring directly into the magical mirror.

"No!" he screamed, scrabbling away until he bumped against the side of the wagon, unable to tear his eyes away. "I gave you a gift! All of you!"

Hutchinson continued to the hold the mirror in front of Penfold's face. The man's screams faded to whimpers, and he curled into a ball. Hutchinson watched in horror as Penfold's face returned to the wrinkled visage he had when he arrived at Abrams House. His black hair faded to iron gray and then went completely white. The man's hands bent into claws and his flesh seemingly melted away. With a final sigh, the skin-covered skeleton collapsed, to move no more.

Hutchinson shook his aching head, unable to believe what he'd just witnessed. Penfold's remains still sat slumped against the side of the wagon. Then he noticed white beads scattered around the body. Were they what had rattled when he'd lifted the jar? He picked one up, examined it, then dropped it with a cry. A human tooth! He picked up another, and another. All teeth. He turned to the shelves and lifted a second jar close to his face. This one contained small bones—finger bones perhaps? A third jar held swatches of hair in all colors.

The man was a monster! The gruesome souvenirs exceeded even Hutchinson's worst nightmares. He lifted his crutch and brought it down on the cursed mirror, over and over until the glass was reduced to shards and the wood case to splinters. He pushed himself up on the crutch and moved the oil lantern to the top of the steps. After sliding down the steps on his belly, he threw the lantern back into the wagon, where the spilled oil quickly ignited.

He hurried away from the wagon as fast as his sore head and the still muddy ground would allow. When he arrived back at Abrams House, he told of Mr. Penfold accidentally dropping the lamp, then pushing him from the wagon before turning back to fight the fire. He'd barely escaped with his life. A column of black smoke rising above the trees lent truth to his tale. Mrs. Forsythe, with tears in her eyes, declared Penfold a godly man till the end, more concerned for others than himself. Hutchinson doubted the former owners of the teeth and bones would agree, but making Penfold out to be a hero drew attention (and suspicion) away from him.

The doctor, who had not in fact been summoned by Penfold, treated Hutchinson's injured head and prescribed a week of bed rest. During that week, Hutchinson had much time to think—many questions and few answers. Had the souls of the men Penfold ushered to their deaths appeared in the mirror when the tinker was forced to look into it? He couldn't be sure. Would Penfold have died from the blow or had Hutchinson killed him with the mirror? In either case, Hutchinson was responsible for the man's death. But he felt no guilt, just relief. And what did the jars of hideous trophies have to do with the mirror's magic, if anything?

Mrs. Forsythe held a grand funeral for the man, fortunately for Hutchinson while he was still on bed rest. She was more taken with Penfold than ever after his "heroic" death. At the week's end, Hutchinson insisted on leaving Abrams House. The place had been fouled by Penfold and he wanted nothing more to do with it. Mrs. Forsythe kindly gave him a small cart and pony for his travels, and he bade farewell to his temporary home.

Hutchinson traveled six miles the first day and set up camp in a sheltered grove. He built a fire and settled his bedroll next to it, feeling lucky to be alive. It would take another week or more to reach his family in the western part of the state. Only his mother and sister remained, and they had no idea he was coming home. He fell asleep smiling at the thought of surprising them.

He was awakened the next morning by something digging into his left hip. Reaching into his pocket, he pulled out a familiar-looking camp mirror. He screamed and threw it into the bushes. The next night, it returned to his pocket. He placed it in front of the cart wheels and ran over it. The next morning it was back. He left it at an inn, threw it in the fire, and tied it to a tree branch. It always came back.

He couldn't carry this cursed object to his family. His sister Margaret was a curious child. What if she found it and opened the cover? Maybe this was delayed justice for his murder of Penfold. In despair, he moved the cart off the path and tied the pony to a tree, sure that someone would find it and rescue the innocent animal. He gathered his few possessions and walked deep into the woods, where he built a fire and prayed for forgiveness.

After his final amen, he reached for the mirror and slid open the cover, hoping that his death would balance the scales of justice and end the curse. He looked into the glass, expecting the final comfort of a glimpse of his mother and sister. Instead, the mirror went black and Penfold's voice filled his head.

The next morning, a newly energized Hutchinson broke camp and walked out of the woods, using the crutch as skillfully as if he'd been born with it. He pulled himself onto the driver's bench of the cart and urged the pony north, toward battlefields filled with dying men.

SALAD COURSE - PLANTS & FUNGI

Recommended Wine: Sauvignon Blanc

OYSTER HUNT

"There," Billy said, pointing to the downed tree. "See those?"

His friend Greg squinted through the sun-dappled pine forest. "The bunch of white-looking things? Yeah."

"That's what we're looking for." Billy pulled the empty plastic bag from his hip pocket and shook it open. "Let's go get 'em."

The two boys trudged toward the decaying tree. Greyish-white pearl oyster mushrooms sprouted in patches on the trunk. This was Billy's first solo foraging expedition, after following his mother on many trips. She'd taught him where to find and how to distinguish the edible wild mushrooms from the dangerous.

"C'mon, Peanut." Greg waved his arm and clicked his tongue toward a small mutt enthusiastically sniffing a pile of deer shit. The dog looked up and trotted after his owner.

The boys carefully broke the fungi from the tree and dropped them in the bag, filling it about a third of the way.

"Let's keep going," said Billy. "My mom will be impressed if we come back with a full bag."

"I've got a better idea," said Greg. "How about we split up and each fill a bag? We can cover twice as much ground. Meet back here in an hour?"

"Okay, here." Billy handed Greg the partially-filled bag, pleasantly surprised that his friend was getting into the thrill of the chase. "Don't pick anything that doesn't look like these."

They pulled out their iPhones and noted the compass coordinates so they could find their way back. Greg and Peanut headed west.

"One hour," repeated Billy, turning to the east. "And stay away from the old commune."

Arcadia Colony had housed a thriving group of hippies back in the 70's. Billy's grandparents had lived there for a while before moving to the outskirts of the town of Grouse Creek. The commune had broken up after five of the residents disappeared and were never seen or heard from again. The founding couple were arrested and held, but ultimately released when no crime could be proved. The land and buildings had been deserted and allowed to fall into ruin.

Over fourty years later, a builder started Paradise Valley near the old site, and his mother had jumped at the chance to return to her roots. She'd only been a toddler when they'd moved away and had nothing but fond memories of her early life at the commune. Billy and Greg's families were the first (and so far only) residents to move in.

Billy moved quietly through the pines and firs, eyes downcast and darting to either side. He squatted to examine another type of mushroom, surprised by its presence. The honey mushroom didn't usually appear until the autumn, and it was only late July. They weren't quite as good as the pearl oysters but were definitely edible. He broke the fruits off and pulled out a second bag to keep the two types separated. Black "shoestrings" clung to the base of each mushroom. These rhizomorphs spread for a long distance underground and made up most of the plant. One specimen was estimated to cover 3.5 miles and was known as the "humongous fungus." Billy smiled every time he thought about that nickname.

By the time he had to head back, he had a full bag of pearl oysters and a half bag of honey mushrooms. His mom would be really pleased, especially if Greg had a full bag of oysters as well. That would be enough to sell at the local farmer's market, along with tomatoes and squash from their large garden.

Billy arrived at the designated meeting spot to find it empty. He double-checked the compass on his phone to make sure he hadn't misread it.

"Greg! Greg! Where are you, man? We're gonna be late."

His phone showed no bars. Not surprising. The only things they used them for out here were the clock and the compass. Billy sighed and started walking in the direction he'd last seen Greg and Peanut. He called out periodically but got no response. Even though he should have kept his eyes up, habit drew them toward the ground. He stopped abruptly and pulled an oyster mushroom from the base of a live tree. That made no sense. Oysters grew on dead and decaying trees, unlike the honeys which fed on live trees. He continued walking past tangled mats of black strings with clumps of honey mushrooms sprouting from them. He cradled the rogue oyster in his right hand, reluctant to mix it with the others but not quite sure why.

The strange oyster was soon trumped by an even stranger sight—oysters sprouting directly from the mats of rhizomorphs, not a honey in sight. He crouched and looked closer. No, wait, in the center of the clump of oysters were the ragged remains of two tiny honeys. His examination was interrupted by a shout.

"Peanut, no! Help! Someone help!"

Billy dropped everything and sprinted toward Greg's voice. He entered a clearing. Crumbled buildings loomed in the distance, overgrown with vines. Shit!

His grandparents had been gardeners at the commune until one of the founders moved them to the kitchens, replacing them with her hand-selected crew. They moved away before the disappearances, realizing that hierarchies lived on even in communal environments. His mother remained fascinated with Arcadia, but nervous about the rumors ranging from poisoning to dismemberment to witchcraft. She had warned Billy away from the place and he'd managed to avoid it. Until now.

He followed the sounds of sobbing until he came upon Greg, kneeling at the edge of a pulsating mass of black strings. In the center of the mass crouched a huge clump of oyster mushrooms. Peanut was being slowly carried toward the oysters with every pulse. The small dog struggled and whined but he was buried in the strings up to his belly.

"I can't reach him!" Greg wailed.

"Get a long stick!" said Billy.

The boys scrabbled on the forest floor, picking up and discarding broken branches. Greg found a suitable stick and kneeled again at the edge of the pulsating mass, holding the stick out as far as he could reach, just above Peanut's head. The dog snapped at the branch, once, twice, before latching on. He leaned back and managed to halt the dog's progress.

"Grab ahold of me!"

Billy wrapped his arms around Greg's waist and pulled. Peanut inched back toward them.

"Again!"

On the third pull, the stick broke. They fell hard and when they looked up, Peanut was disappearing into the mass of oysters. A last whimper and he was gone. The black strings plunged back into the ground except for a circle around the murderous mushrooms. Aside from the overly large clump, the scene looked perfectly normal.

"What just happened?" asked Billy in a shaky voice.

Greg leapt to his feet. "I just lost my fucking dog, that's what happened." His face was red and tearstained. He pointed at Billy. "This is all your fault."

"Greg. Dude." Billy spoke quietly, as if someone might overhear. "We're at the commune."

Greg hesitated and looked around with wild eyes. Then he tightened his lips and began a determined march toward the clump of mushrooms. Billy snatched at the back of his friend's shirt, then pulled his hand back with a hiss. His right palm was covered in small blisters, some already burst, some still intact. The same hand he'd carried the strange oyster in until he heard his friend yell.

"Don't, Greg! There's nothing you can do."

Billy watched helplessly as his friend approached the last place he'd seen his dog, afraid to take a step toward where the fungus had writhed just moments before. Greg reached the giant mushroom mass and hesitated.

"Come back. Hurry!"

Greg nodded and turned around, swiping at tears. He was almost back to where Billy waited when the ground erupted. Black strings covered his feet up to the ankles. His eyes went wide. He gasped and fell to his knees where the busy strings lassoed him. A hissing noise filled the air, as if the rhizomorphs were a bed of snakes.

"Billy! It hurts."

He reached out and Billy leaned in, groping clumsily with his left hand. Their fingers touched, then Greg was tugged backwards.

"Noooo! Make it stop. Do something!"

Billy took a deep breath, stepped one foot on top of the pulsing threads, and just managed to grab Greg's hand and halt his progress. He tried to lift his foot to step back and pull, but the rhizomorphs had already slithered over it. He teetered, waving his free hand for balance before falling into the mat of black strings. Another pulse and both boys were moved toward the clump of oyster mushrooms, hands still joined.

Billy felt a burning sensation where the threads touched him, but it quickly turned to numbness. He turned his head to look at Greg. His friend's eyes were wide with terror.

"Greg! Try to get loose. If we both try, we can do it."

Greg didn't move. His head was almost to the clump of mushrooms. Billy thrashed his arms and legs as if swimming, but his movements were feeble, the numbness overtaking his limbs. He sobbed and closed his eyes. Greg's hand slipped out of his. The pulsing stopped. Billy opened his eyes. He lay a few feet from the clump and his friend was gone. The mushrooms trembled as if excited.

Billy lifted his head. The black strings had retreated, freeing him from their grip. He willed his body to move, but the numbness had turned to paralysis. He dropped his head back and screamed for help, the only thing he could do. After screaming until his voice cracked, he watched daylight fade and eventually dozed off from exhaustion.

He awoke to the sound of people calling his name. He lifted his head and looked at the ground around him. No black strings. He rolled his eyes toward the mass of oyster mushrooms. They weren't moving and, aside from their size, looked normal.

"Here," he croaked. "Over here." A little louder.

A familiar figure broke away from a distant group of people and ran toward him.

"Billy!"

His mother fell to her knees and took his hand.

"Mom! Greg's gone." Sobs of relief momentarily stole his ability to speak.

He looked over his mother's shoulder. Black threads poked up from the ground and wriggled toward them. He inhaled sharply and gasped out one word.

"Run!"

FAMILY TREE

Helen caressed the large woody scar, running her fingers along the dark edges. A full month after the injury, the still-healing wound on the trunk of the massive oak stood out like an angry grimace.

"I'm sorry this happened to you," she whispered.

As an only child, she'd spent many happy hours nestled in the nearly level space between two large limbs, sometimes reading a book and sometimes talking to herself. The oak listened patiently to her childish woes. Even today, at forty-five years old, she often puzzled out problems by way of a conversation with her perennial friend.

Her eyes dropped to the base of the trunk, covered by a roadside memorial that sprung up after the accident. She stuffed a damp, mildewed teddy bear into a trash bag and reached for the plastic-encased photo. It showed a dark-haired girl with a brilliant white smile. Edwina Cox.

A shame. She mashed the photo in on top of the bear. After adding a deflated Mylar balloon printed with 'We Miss You, Eddy,' some ratty plastic flowers, a couple of indecipherable notes with runny ink, and a pale pink ribbon, she cinched the bag.

The oak used to be sixty feet from the road rather than the mere ten feet of today. But that was before Franklin Mill Road had been rerouted and turned into a major thoroughfare. The county paid handsomely for the land, but what had Papa been thinking? Helen had been off at college and returned to a fait accompli. She felt guilty that her education may have cost her friend room to breathe. The oak had since suffered the indignity of having county tree trimmers amputate overhanging limbs. Now it had suffered the indignity of being the immovable object that met an irresistible force.

The next morning, Helen heard the crunch of tires on the gravel driveway, followed by a frantic pounding on her front door. She opened the door to a familiar-looking blonde teenager, fists clenched at her sides and eyes brimming with tears.

"Where is it? What did you do with it?" The girl had been one of the more constant devotees at the tree since the accident.

Helen folded her arms and leaned against the doorjamb. "If you're referring to the 'memorial,' I got rid of it. It's been there a month."

"Eddy was my best friend," the girl wailed. "How will I talk to her now?"

"Young lady, I am sorry for your loss. I allowed the memorial to stay to help you and your friends grieve. And it was beginning to mildew," she added. Helen had scrubbed her hands twice to rid them of the smell after picking up all the trash.

The girl dropped her face into her hands and her shoulders shook. "Eddy will miss me. I have to visit her," she sniffled.

Helen had hoped that by removing the memorial, the stream of mournful-looking teenagers trespassing on her property would stop. Not to mention the scattering of empty beer cans and cigarette butts left in their wake. The grass at the end of the driveway would need replanting at the very least.

"Can't you visit the cemetery?" Helen asked, annoyed at the girl's sense of entitlement.

"She's not there." Hiccupping with sobs, she thrust her finger toward the oak at the end of the driveway. "She's there."

"What do you mean?" Helen still blocked the doorway, but curiosity was overcoming annoyance.

"Eddy told me to come to the tree, so I did." She dropped her eyes and picked at her fingernails, her face still streaked with tears.

Helen took a step back, waved the girl into the foyer, and shut the door. She didn't pay good money to air condition the front yard.

"What do you mean, she 'told you?' Did she 'tell' anyone else?"

"No, she told me after the funeral, in my dream." Eddy's friend looked up. "Her spirit lives in the tree. That's where I go to talk to her."

Helen hesitated, touched by the girl's obvious sincerity. And she was too distraught to drive.

"Why don't you come in?" she asked and led her to the kitchen.

Eddy's friend followed, sniffling and wiping her face. Helen moved a box of Kleenex to the table and motioned to her to sit before re-starting the kettle. The girl slumped in a chair and honked into a tissue.

Helen spooned hot chocolate into a mug, poured in hot water from the kettle, and gave it a brisk stir. She put the mug in front of the girl, picked up her tea and sat in the facing chair. "I'm Helen Todd. And you are...?"

"Abby." The girl poked out a damp hand. "I'm sorry I didn't ask permission. This has never happened to me before." She twirled her hair around her index finger. "Do you still have the stuff?" Her voice brightened.

"I'm afraid it was picked up this morning." Abby's late apology seemed sincere, so Helen tried to soften the blow. "If I'd known someone wanted it…"

Abby ran her fingers down the side of the mottled brown mug. It was one of a set of four fashioned like tree trunks, a curved branch decorated with a single green leaf serving as a handle.

"I come by almost every night," she sniffed, "but last night was my brother's birthday dinner."

"Every *night?*" Helen pressed her lips into a thin line. It was worse than she'd imagined, children trespassing at night. The long winding driveway hid the base of the tree from view, and she was a sound sleeper.

Helen shook her head in disbelief. "That is very danger-ous. It's too close to the road and drivers may not see you at night. Do you want to join your friend?"

Abby pulled back like she'd been slapped, and her lower lip trembled. She shook her head wildly from side to side, then glanced at the kitchen clock and stood abruptly.

"I need to get to school. Sorry to bother you." She bolted out the front door.

Helen spent the rest of the day in her home office. An ar-chitecture degree—earned while her father was busy sell-ing off family land—allowed her to do much of her work from home. And to keep the remaining property intact.

Helen had practically raised herself. Her mother had been fifteen years younger than her father when they married, only eighteen years old and beautiful. After baby Helen was born, her mother handed her off to a series of nannies. Her mother loved the outdoors and spent hours wandering the estate alone. If foul weather rolled in, a servant was sent to fetch her. On fine days she could be found seated in front of an easel at the base of the oak, dabbing paint on a canvas. Recognizing her mental fragility, her father cosseted his wife and gave in to her harmless whims.

Helen had always been a dutiful child and when she was six years old, she assigned herself the care of her mother. She even asked for her own small easel so they could paint together near the oak. She usually enjoyed her mother's lighthearted and cheerful company but constantly worried that she'd fall into one of her "spells" where she ceased to recognize her surroundings. In this state, her mother would either panic and run or curl up in a ball and weep. Helen became adept at calming her and gently leading her back to the house.

When Helen was ten years old, she returned from school one day to find her mother gone. Her father told her he had sent her to a place "where she would be happy." She never saw her mother again and felt guilty that her overwhelming emotion was not grief but relief.

The care of the household, and of her father, continued to be her responsibility as she grew older. When he died suddenly, she discovered she enjoyed being alone with no one depending on her or influencing her decisions. A marriage proposal was sacrificed in favor of her newfound appreciation for finally having complete control of her life.

Eddy's accident had shaken that hard-won control. Removing the memorial *should* put an end to the disruptions, but Abby seemed adamant her dead friend was communicating with her from the oak. The tree had been gravely injured, so why should it offer shelter to its assailant? Helen pushed the foolish thought away. Comforting as it was, the oak was still just a tree.

After dinner, Helen settled into her evening ritual of a book and a glass of wine. But tonight, her thoughts kept drifting to Abby's impossible claim. At 11:00, fortified by an extra glass of wine, she snapped the book closed. Couldn't hurt to make sure the silly girl hadn't returned to pile more trash at the foot of the tree. She picked up a flashlight and pulled on a cardigan.

The flashlight revealed nothing but the wounded oak. No pictures, balloons, teddy bears, dolls, or other detritus. She switched off the light and sat leaning against the trunk, away from the road and shielded from sight. Crickets sang and an occasional car rolled by. The air smelled of rich soil and fresh-cut grass. A cave-like gloom dominated the area beneath the thick canopy.

Over three hundred years old, the tree had been on the property when her great grandfather, Isiah, purchased the land and built the house. It had sheltered generations of

Todd children, who'd frolicked and played under and in its branches. There *had* been the unfortunate incident with Rebeccah, her great aunt, but otherwise the oak was a benevolent and calming presence.

The unaccustomed extra wine combined with the peaceful night caused her to drowse. A sweep of headlights pulled her back to wakefulness. Footsteps crunched on the gravel. Helen froze and held her breath.

"Eddy. I'm here," said a familiar young voice. Abby!

"I missed you," a different female voice said.

Helen whipped her head around. The second voice seemed to be coming from inside the tree. She pulled her cardigan close, pressed her back against the tree, and listened.

"Oh, thank goodness! I was afraid you wouldn't be here. That old bitch took the memorial down."

Helen started. Old bitch?

"She can't come between us, we're best friends," the other voice (Eddy?) said.

Abby let out a sound between a laugh and a sob. "But we can't *do* anything together. Ever again."

"What if I told you we could be together forever?" Eddy asked.

"But how? I'm alive and you're...not."

"Oh, but I am. Just in a different way. If you join me, you'll get to meet my *new* friend, and we'll all be *so* happy."

Enough. Helen pushed herself up and stepped around the tree. No one there but Abby, who gasped and backed away. Helen looked around quickly before grabbing the girl's arms and shaking her.

"I don't know what kind of trick you think you're playing here. You knew I was listening the whole time." She looked around again, searching for the source of the other voice.

"No, no!" Abby shook her head. "I didn't know you were there. You heard her?" The girl's eyes were as big as silver dollars.

Helen let her go. "I bet she doesn't have anything else to say now." She cupped a hand to her ear. "Isn't that right, Eddy?"

Wind rustled the leaves. Crickets chirped. Abby's breath came in gasps.

"Didn't think so." Helen pointed Abby toward her car. "Leave now and I won't press charges. And don't come back."

Helen struggled to sleep that night. Fragments of dreams swirled as she tossed and turned, and she jolted awake at one point, certain she'd heard a female voice speak her name. Images of Eddy's smiling face swapped places with images of Great Aunt Rebeccah's solemn one, both tragically young when they lost their lives.

She spent the morning in her office, still caught in the memories of last night's dreams. The blueprints from the current job blurred before her tired eyes, and she drank an extra cup of coffee.

After lunch, she walked down the driveway to collect the mail. She stopped in front of the oak and her eyes rose to a broad, old stub on the right side of the trunk, fifteen or so feet up. Isiah had cut the branch off after he cut Rebeccah down. Punishing the tree hadn't brought her back. Nor would a hundred tacky memorials bring Eddy back. A cough from behind startled her out of her meditation.

"Helen, Miss Todd?" Abby stood in the driveway, her back pressed against her gray Prius.

Helen frowned. She hadn't heard the girl pull up. "I thought I told you not to come back."

"Could you come over here, please?" Abby asked. "I want to apologize and explain."

Helen folded her arms but didn't move. "I'm listening."

Abby glanced nervously at the oak while twirling her hair around her index finger. "Can we go up to the house?"

Helen decided to hear her out. They walked up the driveway in silence. The closer they got to the house, the calmer the girl seemed.

"This is getting to be a habit," Helen said, putting a steaming mug of hot chocolate on the kitchen table.

"I'm sorry about last night, Helen. I'm sorry I called you...."

"An old bitch?"

Abby flushed. "Yeah. And it really *was* Eddy who was talking, not me. You've got to believe me." She met Helen's eyes.

"Let's say I do believe you. Why did you come back last night?"

"I had to see if she was still there. I used to look at her picture while we talked, and it almost felt normal." Abby gripped the mug, her knuckles white. "We always just talked about our friends, school and stuff." She giggled nervously. "It made me feel like she was still here. But last night, I'm really glad you were there." Her voice quivered.

"Why is that?"

"Because I think she wants to kill me!" Abby almost shrieked the words. "What else could 'join her' mean? Even if you hadn't been there, I would've run away. You don't have to worry about me going near the tree ever again."

"Glad to hear it."

The girl's pale face and dark circles under her eyes showed that she hadn't had a restful night either. Helen felt a tug of sympathy.

Abby took a deep breath. "And I don't think you should go near it either. If you can hear Eddy, she could hurt you too."

Helen suppressed a chuckle. "Abby, she can't hurt you, and she certainly can't hurt me. But I am happy you won't be creeping around the end of my driveway at night anymore."

Recalling the previous night's conversation between "the girls," a niggling suspicion surfaced in Helen's mind.

"Eddy didn't happen to tell you the name of her 'new friend,' did she?" She hoped the question sounded casual.

Abby shook her head, looking forlorn. "That was the first time she mentioned it. Sounds like she's happier with her new friend."

Helen rested her hand on the seated girl's shoulder. "I think you should follow her lead and look for a new best friend. I know you won't be visiting the tree anymore." She paused, then surprised herself. "But you're welcome to call me if you want to talk."

She recited her number and the girl entered it into her cell phone. Before leaving, Abby opened her arms and stepped forward. Helen returned the hug, surprising herself for a second time that morning.

Helen returned to her routine but found herself distracted. Her eyes drifted to the top of the built-in bookshelves in the office. There, carefully preserved, was a display of family history—the old Bible, along with journals and diaries from various ancestors. Her father spoke often of his plans to write a family history, but a sudden heart attack had taken him just before his sixtieth birthday.

She pulled down the heavy, leather-bound Bible. It opened with a crack and a musty smell. A sepia photograph of a solemn-looking Rebeccah was tucked between the first two pages. Partway down a list written inside the cover was her entry, born August 14, 1901, died March 2, 1919. Seventeen years old, the same age as Eddy.

Helen closed the Bible and reached for a small journal, Rebeccah's diary. The only reason it survived Isiah's wrath after her death was because Jessie, the housekeeper's daughter, had hidden it. She turned to the last page.

March 2, 1919

Dear Diary,

Daddy has forbidden me from seeing Charles! It's not fair! He says it's because his family isn't "at our level" in society. What a snob! If Mother were alive, I'm sure she'd love Charles. He's handsome and kind and respectful, and he loves me! And I love him too!

But I have a plan to get Daddy to change his mind. I was daydreaming in the branches of the oak yesterday when a thought popped into my head. What if I fell? What if I was injured? Daddy would do anything to forestall that. This afternoon before he leaves the mill, I'll send a note, begging him to come to the oak to talk. Life or death, I'll say.

According to Helen's father, Rebeccah had sent Jessie to deliver the note, then took her pony cart to the oak. She fashioned a noose, looped it around a thick branch, and stood in the cart to await her father. But before he arrived, the pony bolted. Rather than a clean and fast broken neck, Rebeccah strangled slowly, her feet only inches above the ground. Isiah had been detained at work and arrived half an hour after he'd been expected home. He found the pony nuzzling Rebeccah's lifeless body as though trying to wake her. After he cut her down, he shot the unfortunate pony.

Helen rested her elbows on the desk and leaned into her hands, rubbing her eyes. Rebeccah had hatched her plan while seated, alone, in the oak. By all reports, her pony had been a solid, calm animal until that day. What had really happened? Eddy had also been alone when she drove her car into the oak. Abby had told her that Eddy was a particularly careful driver, but no one knew what really happened then either. The only constant between the two events was the tree.

She pulled her thoughts back from that senseless path. Two accidents, nearly 100 years apart, had nothing to do with each other.

The following week, Abby called Helen to tell her about a new friend she'd met at school, an exchange student from France. The girl never mentioned Eddy. Helen felt like a weight had been lifted—she would get her old life back.

In celebration that evening, Helen opened a bottle of Cabernet Sauvignon she'd been saving for a special occasion. Engrossed in her book, she lost track of the time. She also lost track of the wine. She jammed the cork into the neck of the nearly empty bottle and moved it out of sight. The clock showed ten minutes to midnight, but she was wide awake. A bright full moon hung suspended over the oak, lighting it up like a holiday display. She opened the door and started down the driveway. A faint rumble of thunder sounded in the distance.

She'd been unable to shake the feeling that the two girls' deaths were somehow related. Not exactly sure what to expect, she hoped for an answer, even if only through the emotions that the oak had always elicited from her. But she *had* heard a "voice" from the tree, so maybe Eddy would talk to her, tell her more about how the accident happened.

"Hello. Is anyone there?" Her words sounded ridiculous in the empty night.

"Hello, Helen," said a young woman. Not Eddy.

Helen's voice dried in her throat. She circled the tree, sweeping her eyes down the road, then toward the house. Completely alone. The closest neighbor was over a mile away.

She swallowed hard, then croaked "Aunt Rebeccah?" feeling sick and excited at the same time.

"Yes, Helen," the voice responded. "I'm happy we can finally speak. I watched you grow up. I've been witness to many things over the years."

"But how? Why are you still here?"

Rebeccah laughed. "I wish I knew. I've been here in the oak, mute and alone since that dreadful day."

"Did you mean to kill yourself?" Helen blurted it out, eager to get an answer from the one person who knew exactly what happened.

"Of course not! A branch cracked and fell and startled Stubby." Rebeccah sighed. "I don't know why it bothered him so, but I do wish Papa hadn't shot him."

As if to confirm the story the wind picked up, making the oak's large canopy sway and creak as large branches rubbed against one another. Helen paused to let the fact that she was talking to a disembodied voice sink in. A disembodied voice belonging to a deceased relative.

"So why didn't you talk to me before?" Helen asked. "You said you watched me grow up. I practically lived in this tree as a child." Had it been Rebeccah she sensed when she imagined the tree communicating with her?

"All I know is when Edwina died her spirit stayed here and joined mine. And we could speak! The accident not only gave me voice, but a companion."

"So, you *are* Eddy's new friend."

"Oh yes. I'm most grateful to her. Edwina is a lovely young lady."

"So, is Eddy happy?" Helen asked.

"She misses her best friend, but she'll be fine." Rebeccah laughed bitterly. "This odd existence does require some adjustment. Luckily for her, I can serve as her guide."

"Tell her Abby misses her but is adjusting as well. She has a new friend at school." Helen felt relieved she could tell Abby the threat from her late friend seemed to have gone away.

"I will. Edwina will be pleased. She wants nothing but good things for Abigail."

The wind gusted again, whipping Helen's hair into her face. She pushed it back with one hand, blinking as dust from the base of the tree swirled upward. There had been no rain in over a month. A louder rumble of thunder predicted the end of the dry spell.

"To celebrate our meeting, I'd like to give you a gift," Rebeccah said. "A family heirloom. I'm sure you'll recognize it."

"A gift?" Helen shook her head. This evening was becoming progressively more surreal.

"Look inside the gash in the trunk. See the gold chain?"

Helen moved closer. In the base of the wound nearly at ground level, moonlight reflected off something shiny. Her heart kicked into overdrive. There had been nothing there before.

"It belonged to your mother."

For the first time in years, memories of her mother flooded Helen's mind. She had loved jewelry, but her favorite piece had been a ruby pendant on a braided gold chain. A piece which had originally belonged to Rebeccah.

"The pendant? But she never took it off. How could it be here?"

Rebeccah sighed. "Once you retrieve it, all will become clear. Go ahead. It belongs to you now."

Helen hesitated. She had just "met" Rebeccah, but she did have a lifelong friend to help her decide what to do. Stepping toward the oak, she rested both hands lightly on the trunk, closed her eyes, and waited. A familiar feeling of calm and well-being settled over her. Reassured, she knelt and thrust her hand into the base of the scar, grabbed the chain, and pulled gently. Stuck. She began to dig away the loose bark. It was oddly soft and yielding, like shredded cork. Burrowing deep into the opening she felt the pendant at the end of the chain, pinched it between her index and middle fingers, and began to withdraw her hand.

Once the pendant cleared the wood, she grasped it firmly and continued to pull, but the chain was still stuck. She dug again in the loose bark and felt something caught on the end of the chain. Curling her fingers around the object, she brought it out and opened her hand. Resting on her palm was a bone, a vertebra large enough to be human, with the chain looped through it. She gasped and threw it to the ground, necklace and all.

When her father had sent her mother away, Helen hadn't questioned him. Nor had she questioned the new mulch around the base of the oak, roped off for over a month to "help it heal from the drought" he'd said. And even though there hadn't been a lot of rain, the oak had thrived after that, with more young branches and a leafier canopy.

She lunged forward and began tearing at the base of the tree with both hands, ignoring the pain from torn fingernails. "No, no, no, no, no!"

She felt a bundle of small sticks in the shredded bark, pulled them out, and dropped them next to the necklace. Finger bones. Sitting back on her heels, she lifted her head and wailed with loss and betrayal. As if in sympathy, the next roll of thunder brought the first drops of rain to blend with her tears.

"Why?" Helen's voice shook. "Why? She never hurt anyone!"

This couldn't be possible. Her demanding father—what could her gentle mother have done to deserve such a fate? And Helen had accepted his story without question, never even asking to visit her mother. Anger, guilt, loss, and betrayal leached the strength from her limbs and she collapsed, clutching the pitiful remains to her chest.

Neither Rebeccah nor the oak answered her plea. Wind drove the now heavy rain into her, each drop feeling like a small bullet. Branches creaked and groaned their complaints as the wind tossed them around to an accompaniment of crashes of thunder. Lightning strobed overhead, replacing the steady glow of the moon.

Belatedly aware of the danger she was in, Helen scooped up the pendant and bones and staggered to her feet. She had only taken a few steps away from the oak before she was enveloped in a bright flash. Pain knifed through her from her right shoulder to her left leg and she fell to the ground.

She struggled to breathe. Her heart skipped and raced and skipped again before settling into a choppy rhythm. Still gasping for breath and with eyes closed in pain, she dragged herself forward with her good left arm, hoping she was moving toward the house. Her hand struck rough bark and told her she'd miscalculated. Weak and defeated, she pulled herself up and leaned against the trunk of the oak.

"You'll protect me, won't you?" slurred Helen. Her mouth didn't seem to be working properly. "I've always protected you."

The oak remained implacable.

"Rebeccah?"

Silence. This was a nightmare. Why hadn't she just gone to bed?

"I loved you," she whispered to the unfeeling tree, tears spilling from her eyes.

She gasped as the trunk vibrated against her back, a conduit for the true feelings of the oak. It overflowed with feelings—those of cruelty and pleasure, like a sadistic child pulling the legs off an insect. If the oak could have communicated aloud, it would have laughed.

Helen threw herself away from the traitorous tree, barely getting her good arm down to prevent falling on her face. Using her left arm and right leg, she began an awkward crawl toward the driveway. Reaching the gravel after what seemed like hours, she paused to catch her breath and looked back at the tree. The scar in the trunk leered back.

A gust of wind roared out of the dying storm and she heard a loud crack. An impossibly heavy object crashed onto the back of her neck, pinning her to the driveway. Excruciating pain was followed by a merciful blackness rolling across her vision. When she came to, she could not move—arms, legs, not even a finger. A huge branch lay across her back, pinning her to the driveway. Her breathing slowed and she began to gasp. It was like sucking air through a straw.

Helen closed her eyes. Breathe in. She saw Rebeccah's face, eyes bulging and bloodshot, purple tongue lolling from her once pretty mouth. Breathe out. Eddy's face, blood running from her split forehead, her brain visible through the shattered skull. Breathe in. She saw her own face twisted in pain and disbelief.

Consciousness of the physical world faded. The last thing she felt was gravel cutting into her cheek and blood filling her mouth. The last thing she heard was the laughter of young women.

PALATE CLEANSER - EVIL CHILDREN

Recommended Wine: Albarino

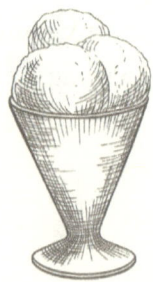

AMAZING PATSY

"Granny, they did it again," Patsy wailed. Her light blonde hair dripped with a sticky orange liquid. Fanta.

"Come here, child." I motioned her to the farmhouse sink and dunked her head under running water, combing her hair with my fingers. "Kids were mean to me when I was your age. Your Mama too, God rest her soul."

"Why do they hate us?" Her pale blue eyes begged for an answer. At eight, she was three years older than I'd been when I heard the Story. It was time. Past time.

With a towel wrapped around her wet hair, she looked like a miniature version of her mother, Ellen. My heart ached at the memory of my daughter covering her bald head with colorful turbans, pretending that she was fine, all the while wasting away. Patsy, a wise child, played along. I delayed telling her the Story in the hope of preserving just a few more years of childhood and innocence. Enough of those years had been stolen by her mother's illness and lingering death. I'd raised Patsy since she was five years old.

We faced each other across the kitchen table, she with a mug of hot chocolate, me with a cup of coffee sweetened with a shot of Jack Daniels for courage.

"Honey, you know how I always tell you you're special?"

She smiled. "All grannies say that."

"That may well be, and I'm guilty as charged. But you really are special, just like your Mama was and like I am. All the way back to my Great Granny Maude." I covered her small hand with mine. "You're going to be the sixth Charmer in the family."

She furrowed her brow. "What IS that? How does it work? Charmer? Will it work on them mean Wilkins sisters?"

I smiled and held up both hands. "Whoa, give me a chance to tell you! It doesn't work on people."

I took a long swallow from my mug, inhaling the sweet smell of Jack Daniels and feeling its warmth slide down my throat. My granddaughter's reaction to the Story would guide both our futures.

"One girl in each generation of our family is able to charm Bloody Cane Toads."

She shook her head. "Miss McCarthy says Bloody Cane Toads aren't real, someone made 'em up to scare kids away from Big Cypress Swamp."

"Teachers aren't as smart as they think they are. Sometimes old knowledge is the best knowledge."

Patsy looked skeptical.

"My Great Granny Maude was the first Charmer. She lived in the old homestead."

The old homestead was right on the edge of the Swamp. Nothing more than a shotgun shack, constantly-open windows served as air conditioning. Screens added by my father kept bugs out, but constant heat pressed down like a soggy blanket.

"Great Granddaddy Ralph worked the cane fields. His boss got the bright idea to bring in a new kind of Cane Toad from South America. Now, you know how big regular Cane Toads are."

"Big as Daddy's hand!" She put her fingers and thumbs together to outline how big she remembered his hands were. When Ellen had gotten sick, Patsy's Daddy had up and disappeared.

"That's right, honey." I didn't discourage her talking about her Daddy, but I didn't encourage it either.

"Well, these new toads were half again as big, and meaner. Some folks said they were part piranha. The company brought 'em in to eat the pests in the cane fields. And boy did they do the job—they ate mice, lizards, small frogs, birds, as well as the cane beetles. The new toads not only had poison in their skin, but poison glands near their mouths as well. And they had two rows of tiny pointed teeth like the edge of a serrated knife. Maybe they were part-piranha." I laughed, and Patsy laughed with me though it wasn't really funny. Nerves I guess.

I continued. "Eventually the toads ran out of food and moved on."

"Moved on?" asked Patsy. She wore a chocolate moustache from her drink. I motioned to her and she knuckled her hand across her mouth, leaving a small smear on her left cheek.

"Yes, but it took a while for the company to realize that. The toads moved at night and rested during the day, so no one saw them travel. Another difference from regular Cane Toads, besides being bigger and having a dark red belly."

"You mean a Bloody belly."

"Folks only added 'Bloody' after the first incident. Scarier."

Her eyes widened but she kept quiet.

"Great Granddaddy Ralph was the first to see a knot of 'em. That's what a group of toads is called, a knot," I added in response to her puzzled look. "It was January, so it got dark earlier. He and his partner, Billy, were walking out of the fields after their shift when they saw them. Ralph said it looked like an ocean of enormous toads covering the path, hopping over and on top of each other. The men froze twenty feet away. A small swamp deer leapt from the cypresses, landed in the middle of the knot, then let out a scream. Ralph said he'd never heard a deer scream like that. The toads latched onto the deer's belly and legs, pulling it down until it disappeared under a thrashing blanket of warty bodies. A noise like rubbing sandpaper filled the air as they pushed each other aside to feed. In minutes, the deer was nothing but bones and the toads moved away from the men into the swamp."

"Weren't they scared?" Patsy hugged herself and shivered.

"Of course they were. And they were lucky, too. The toads weren't interested in them, at least not that day."

"Was that when people started to call the toads 'Bloody?'"

"Not yet. When Ralph and Billy reported what they'd seen, the boss didn't believe them. Said they must have had some 'shine in their lunch buckets." I poured myself another coffee, with a generous dollop of Jack Daniels.

"Ralph invited Billy over for supper the next week. While Maude was cleaning up the kitchen, the men stepped into the backyard for cigars. She heard a horrible ruckus and ran to the door where she saw giant toads covering Billy to the waist, with more climbing him like he was a tree. A couple of them spattered in blood hopped off with big chunks of torn flesh in their mouths and more climbed on. Billy screamed 'Get 'em off, get 'em off!' while Ralph swatted at the toads with a shovel, knocking one off only to have two more latch on. Ralph's feet and ankles were covered with toads. He stood on one leg to shake them off the other and almost fell, finally pushing himself back up with the shovel and limping toward Billy.

Maude didn't know what to do. Then she knew exactly what to do, like she was following an order from God. She started singing."

I broke into the song she sang that night. "Amazing Grace, how sweet the sound...."

"Singing?" Patsy scrunched her face. "That wouldn't do any good."

"It was the best thing, the only thing, she could have done. The toads fell off both men, faced Maude, and sat in front of her like well-behaved schoolchildren. Still singing, she walked slowly into the cypresses with the knot following. When she returned singing the last line, 'Than when we've first begun,' there wasn't a toad in sight."

The child's mouth hung open. "What happened to Great Granddaddy Ralph and Billy?"

I shook my head. "Billy died. Great Granddaddy Ralph never worked again. The docs had to amputate his left foot to save him, and he walked with crutches the rest of his life."

"Did anyone try to hunt the toads?"

"Nobody believed the story. Then the tests came back as a match for Cane Toad poison and the bites were the right size for Bloody Cane Toads. But they still didn't believe that Maude had charmed them away, said the toads must have left on their own."

Patsy rested her chin on her hands. "So, anyone could get rid of the toads just by singing 'Amazing Grace?'"

"It's not the song, honey, it's the singer. One of the nurses got to talking about what happened and the story grew. Sure enough, some fool had to test it. Cissy Woodburn went into the Swamp on a dare from her sorority sisters. They heard her start to sing 'Amazing Grace,' but when the song turned to screams they ran for their lives. Never found a trace of Cissy."

"How did Granny Maude know she had to sing?"

"It came over her, like a vision, she said. She could no sooner have stopped herself than she could have stopped a runaway train."

"Did she keep singing 'Amazing Grace' to the toads?"

"Yes. Yes, she did. She said the song had been given to her and it wasn't her place to change it. But when she taught my granny how to charm, she told her to be open to receiving her own song. And that's how it's been ever since."

"You sing 'Imagine' all the time. Is that your toad-charming song?"

I shrugged. "That's what I was given. Good thing I like it."

I'd been thrilled when I received that song—it was my favorite at the time. Although sometimes I do wish I'd been given a backup.

Patsy bounced in her chair. All the singing she'd heard from me and her Mama now made sense. "Was Mama's song 'I'll Stand By You?'"

"It was, but she didn't really like it. She kept trying new ones but had to fall back to the one she'd been given."

"I hope I get 'Hello,' I'll never get sick of it." She thought for a minute, then looked up at me with a solemn expression. "But no one ever sees the Toads. Are they even alive anymore?"

"You'll see tonight."

"Tonight?" Her big grin was like the sun coming out from behind the clouds.

A less special child would have been terrified, but Patsy was excited. Since Ellen died, I'd carried out the inherited duties by myself. But Ellen hadn't been as strong a Charmer as me, even before she got sick. Patsy reminded me of myself at her age. She would be a natural.

That night I strode into Big Cypress Swamp, hand-in-hand with my granddaughter. She screamed in terror at her first sight of the knot, while I admired the undulating ocean of grays, greens, and browns, with the occasional flash of a red belly. When a toad touched her bare foot, her screaming changed to a single held note—D. Then the note rose to a G, and the beautiful sounds of 'Amazing Grace' poured forth.

I remained silent with tears streaming, nearly breathless with pride. The knot turned its focus to Patsy as she completed her song. I'll never forget her look of complete elation. The flash of self-importance I also saw worried me, though. I'd felt the same when I first learned to Charm, and it had led to an unspeakable act.

"I wish it had been 'Hello,'" she said as we walked out of the swamp.

"You should be proud to receive 'Amazing Grace.' Granny Maude must be looking out for you." I swallowed hard to rid myself of the lump in my throat.

"Don't like hymns." She kicked at the dirt, then gave me a determined look. "Granny, I want to practice, even if I don't like the song. Can we do this again tomorrow?"

After a month, I felt confident she could handle this as my partner. She insisted on going to the Swamp every night, even when she was tired from school. I agreed, but only if she kept up with her homework. As I'd suspected, the toads responded to her like she was their Mama. One night while she was still singing, I broke into my Charming song. A few toads hopped toward me, but most remained mesmerized by the strong voice coming from the small girl.

I told her about Sheriff Gainer. There'd been a Sheriff Gainer in town since Maude and Ralph's time. The job seemed as much a legacy for the Gainers as Charming toads was for us. Sheriff Gainer contacted us whenever there was a need for 'toad relocation,' and thus kept both the incidents and the rumors to a minimum.

The better Patsy got at Charming toads, the more confidence she gained. She stopped coming home crying about the mean Wilkins sisters, and in fact, made friends with them. They really were nice girls when you got to know them, always called me "ma'am." The sisters were fascinated with Patsy and mimicked her singing, filling the house with a chorus of sweet girlish voices singing that great hymn.

When she wanted to picnic near the Swamp with her new best friends, I didn't object. Patsy had matured so since taking on the mantle of Charmer. Besides, the toads didn't come out during the day and she could keep them all safe. The girls always returned from their outings laughing and holding hands and seemed to have a wonderful time.

Late this afternoon the three girls went off to play, as usual. Patsy returned alone and told me the sisters walked straight home since they were late for piano lessons.

"It was a great day, Granny, best ever!" With her face flushed pink and her pale blue eyes shining, she was the most beautiful little girl in the world.

She skipped into the back yard to play with her new puppy. The older dog, Silas, had slipped his leash a couple weeks ago while Patsy was walking him near the Swamp and had never come home. I was sure a gator had gotten him, and she'd been inconsolable until I brought Rufus home.

The phone rang.

"Mrs. Wilkins, how are you? No, the girls left here directly." My heart starting racing as pieces fell into place. Silas had been old, and Patsy complained he was no fun anymore. I looked out the window to watch my granddaughter playing chase with Rufus like she hadn't a care in the world.

"Are you sure they didn't stop for ice cream? I see. I'll let you know if I hear anything."

I hung up the phone and leaned against the wall, fighting a dizzy spell. Memories of Patsy's Daddy flashed before me, his terrified eyes begging me to save him as a toad latched onto his tongue, cutting him off in mid-scream. After the toads covered him completely, I'd returned home to fix dinner for my daughter and granddaughter.

I walked to the back door on shaky legs and stopped to steady my breathing. Pasting on a smile, I pushed open the screen and stepped onto the porch.

"Patsy, honey. We need to talk."

AN ECHO OF MURDER

The summer Daddy went off to fight in Vietnam, the summer I turned eleven, I found out that Granny wasn't really my Granny.

Me and Mama had gone to Heron Lake to clean up the house that Granny left Mama when she died the year before. The plan was to stay for a few weeks to keep our minds off Daddy and the war. We finished the cleaning and Mama sprawled out on the dock, listening to the radio and smoking Salems. I went back to the house to fetch my book and noticed Mama had left the attic stairs pulled down. So, of course I had to climb up and take a look, especially since she'd told me not to.

There wasn't much up there but dust and old cardboard boxes. I poked around, opening the boxes and peering in. I was about to give up when I noticed a shoebox tucked inside one of the bigger boxes. It was marked "Mary Margaret" in Granny's spidery handwriting. Mama's real name was Mary Margaret, but she hated it and went by Meg. I pulled the lid off and saw an old photo, a yellowed, official-looking paper, and a stack of newspaper clippings. I didn't have enough time to go through everything before Mama came looking for me, so I tucked the box under my arm, hurried down the stairs, and stashed it in my bedroom closet.

"You sure took your time," Mama said, peering over her sunglasses as I stepped back onto the dock. She lifted her can of Schlitz and took a swallow.

"Found it," I said, waving my copy of *Charlie and the Chocolate Factory*.

The rest of the afternoon, I tried to concentrate on the book, but kept thinking about that mysterious box. I begged off at 8:30 that evening, saying I was tired from all the cleaning and wanted to go to bed. In the dark, I lay awake for an hour, listening to Mama move around the house. Finally, she stumbled up the stairs and I heard her swear, then her bedroom door closed. I waited ten more minutes, then pulled the shoebox from the closet along with my flashlight.

I focused the dim beam of light on the photo, a small girl frowning at the camera —three years old, maybe four? I flipped it over and read "Mary Margaret, 1935" on the back. I took a closer look. Why would Granny hide this? Setting the picture aside, I reached for the newspaper clippings. Bold headlines leapt out —Murderous Mother

Captured. Trial Date Set for Rita Mueller. Mueller Denies Charges, Blames Mysterious Intruder. What Does the Baby Remember? Curious, I stacked the clippings in date order and began to read.

In 1935, Rita Mueller murdered four of her five children by slitting their throats. Before succumbing to her mother's knife, the nine-year-old girl hid her three-year-old sister, saving her life. Mr. Mueller had come home early and unwittingly interrupted his wife's killing spree. Rita Mueller ran away before locating her youngest daughter's hiding place. When the cops caught her the next day, she claimed to have gotten the bloodstains on her clothes while holding and trying to save her children. She blamed a burglar for the crimes, but police found no signs of a break-in. The three-year old, when asked who had hurt her brothers and sisters, said one word. "Mommy." The little girl's name was Mary Margaret. My heart skipped a beat.

I picked up the photo again. Had it been taken before the murders, or after?

Placing it back in the box, I picked up the thick, yellowed document. "Adoption Agreement" marched in bold, black letters across the top. The child's name was listed as Mary Margaret Mueller. Attached to the back of the document was a single, much older sheet of paper. I held the flashlight close and moved it left to right, following the faded lettering. It said that four-year old Mary Margaret Mueller was being "surrendered" (like she was a stray dog or something) to the Sisters of Mercy Orphanage. The signature at the bottom read "Stanley Mueller." How could he do that? My mind went to my Daddy, who would never, ever give me up. I was his special girl.

I flipped back to the front page. Mary Margaret had been five years old when Richard and Betsy Coleman adopted her. My Granny and Papap. Mama had spent a whole year in an orphanage.

I dropped the documents on the bed, heart racing, my world blown wide open. Swallowing hard, I returned to the news clippings.

Rita Mueller was hanged in 1936. The blurry newspaper photo showed her being led to the executioner. Her face looked familiar, her light-colored wavy hair a lot like mine. A copy of my own eyes, and Mama's, stared angrily back from the photo as she struggled with the men holding her arms, a fighter till the end. Maybe Mr. Mueller hadn't been able to stand having his surviving daughter around because she looked too much like her mother.

I repacked the shoebox, slid it under the bed, and lay staring at the ceiling. This explained so much. Mama was as ordinary as ordinary could be. Me, on the other hand, I was exceptional. I always just figured I got it from Daddy, but it turned out Mama may have had something to do with it after all. We'd learned about genetics in science class —what were the chances of having blue eyes if one parent had brown eyes and the other had blue, that kind of stuff. But I guess personalities could get passed along, too.

When I was four, I accidentally broke my turtle, Tommy. I didn't know you couldn't just press the top and bottom of the shell back together once you pulled them apart. But it was really interesting to see all the shiny, wet innards. I poked at them with a stick until Tommy stopped moving, then took him to the woods and told Mama he must have run away.

For my sixth birthday, Daddy bought me a guinea pig. I remember Mama's worried look when I opened the box and a whiskered nose poked out but didn't think much of it at the time. I named him Buster, and he made it a few months. But when Buster bit me for no reason, I threw him against the wall. He didn't move after that, so I carried him into the field behind the house and opened his belly with a fountain pen and paper-cutting scissors. Not much different from the turtle. I made sure to bury what was left of him. Then I told Mama I had taken him outside to eat some grass and that he hopped away when I wasn't looking. She spent a long time searching for him and seemed pretty upset. I didn't even know she liked Buster that much.

Daddy started taking me fishing when I was seven, even though I'm a girl. He said I was his son and daughter all rolled up in one. I learned how to use his Imperial knife to cut fishing wire and get hooks out. The knife had a regular blade and a saw blade for scaling, and a mother-of-pearl handle with a brass fish embedded in it. The blades folded into the handle and fit in my hand just perfect. It was beautiful.

Before Daddy left for Vietnam, he gave me that knife. From then on, I never went anywhere without it. Mama tried to get me to leave it behind before we came to the lake, but because I planned to fish, she couldn't really come up with a good reason. She acted nervous when I played with it, whittling sticks and whatnot. I always thought it was because she was afraid I'd cut myself with it, but now I wonder.

The next morning, a hard slap to the face woke me up. Mama grabbed my shoulders and shook me.

"Where is it, Dede? I know you took it."

I started crying, not having to try very hard to look upset. "What do you mean, Mama?"

"The shoebox with my name on it." She shook me again. "I told you to stay out of the attic." She scanned the room —her gaze dropped to the floor. With her toe, she nudged the box sticking out from under the bed, then reached down and snatched it up. "How much did you read?"

I pressed myself against the wall, as far away from her as I could get. My shoulders heaved and my voice shook. "A...all of it. But Mama, you didn't do anything wrong."

Her face fell and she looked like a deflated balloon. "I know, sweetie. But I didn't want you to know about Rita."

"You mean my grandmother?"

She clenched her jaw and spoke through gritted teeth. "That woman didn't deserve to have kids or be called mother. Granny is, was, your grandmother." She rubbed her face wearily. "God, I wish she was here. She'd know what to do."

"Do? Why do we have to do anything?" I inched across the bed and put my hand on her arm. "I know about gr...Rita now. I won't tell anyone, I promise." A thought flitted through my mind. "Does Daddy know?"

"Your daddy knows I was adopted." Mama sighed and stared out the window, eyes unfocused. "Granny told him she didn't know anything about my parents."

"So, Granny lied to Daddy."

I was relieved that Daddy didn't know. I'd hate to think he was keeping something from me.

She slid her arm around me and pulled me close. "It's better this way, Dede. I wish I didn't remember Rita, or what happened. I wish Granny and Papap had been my real parents. I'm sorry I got so mad. I've been afraid of you finding out. But just because Rita was evil doesn't mean I am. Or that you are, either."

I pulled away from her. "I am not evil."

"Oh, I didn't say you were, baby," she said, but a shadow crossed her face. "I thought you might be worried about it. Come over here." She held out her arms. I snuggled close and smelled comforting traces of cigarette smoke and Chanel No. 5 —Mama's special scent.

"What do you remember about her?"

"Not much, baby. She was always yelling at us. That day, I thought it was just more of the usual until Steffie shoved me in the closet and told me to stay still and shut up. I peeked out through the slats and saw..." She shivered. "Never mind what I saw. Rita was wicked and got what she deserved. I got a better life with your Granny and Papap, and now I have you." She kissed the top of my head and squeezed me tight. "Now, get dressed and I'll make pancakes."

After breakfast, I cleared the table. The windows hung open with a warm morning breeze moving the curtains. The weather was perfect.

"Can we take the boat out and go fishing?" I asked.

"I was going to do some more sunbathing," she said, frowning and drumming her fingers on the Formica table.

I rubbed my face where she'd slapped me earlier.

"But it is a beautiful day," she said, with a nervous smile. "And I can get sun on the boat just as well."

Mama hated fishing, but she liked fresh fish and boat rides. She put on her sun hat and packed a picnic lunch, filling a cooler with Schlitz and some RC colas for me. I brought my rod and tackle box, not forgetting Daddy's fishing knife. Mama's cooler still had plenty of room for any fish I caught. I hopped into the rowboat and she handed me the picnic basket, hanging onto the cooler as she stepped in and settled onto the middle seat.

"I'll row out and you row back," she said, picking up the oars.

"Deal."

That was the deal she usually made with Daddy. I'd been practicing my rowing, and knew if you used your legs and back, you didn't have to be super strong.

We ate lunch. Mama had put a couple extra slices of Wonder bread in the basket so I could roll it into balls for bait. I had some spinners, but the fish in Heron Lake really liked bread. By the time I cast my first line, Mama was finishing her second Schlitz. She was drinking a whole lot more beer than she did when Daddy was around. I think she missed him. She smoked a lot more cigarettes, too, sometimes lighting one off the other.

Before long, Mama was down to two beers. I slipped a couple of bluegills into the cooler alongside the remaining cans, and she giggled.

"Don't you drink my beer, fish!" she said to the cooler, and giggled again.

By just after four o'clock, I'd caught two crappies to go with the bluegills, so we had plenty of fish for dinner. I'd have to clean them, of course. The only time Mama touched fish was to bread them and drop them in sizzling Crisco.

"Ready to head back?" I asked.

Mama was dozing with her head on her chest, sun hat hiding her face. Her last can of beer rested on the seat next to her with her hand around it.

"Mama!"

Her head jerked up. She peered at me with glassy eyes, then lifted her Schlitz. "Here's to my tough little girl. I love you, sweetie." She stood to change places with me but missed her footing and fell backward. Her hat flew off, her head crunched against the oar lock, and she crashed into the bottom of the boat.

I hung onto the sides of the rocking boat and stared, my heart pounding. She wasn't moving. I crawled toward her.

"Mama?"

I stuck my hand behind her head. It was wet and sticky. I drew back blood-covered fingers. She groaned but her eyes stayed shut. I licked my fingers. They tasted like pennies.

What would Rita do?

I rowed the boat to a secluded inlet.

It really doesn't take much to tie up a drunk, unconscious woman. Even a child can do it. I looked at Mama lying there, trussed up like a pig, only instead of an apple I'd stuffed an oily rag in her mouth. I had the same feeling of power as when I'd thrown Buster into the wall, and later when I'd caught that stray cat. I'd learned a lot from the cat —he lasted a couple of days. But now I knew where my power came from. I would make my grandmother, my real grandmother, proud.

I started on Mama's arms, pressing the blade of Daddy's knife deep into the soft skin between her wrist and elbow, making neat lines and watching her blood well from the cuts. I stuck my finger in the blood and licked it, then lowered my head and sucked on her arm. Salty and delicious. She woke up and made squealing noises through the rag.

"There you go, Mama. Just cleaning up my mess." I licked my lips. "You always tell me to clean up after myself."

She shook her head, the whites of her eyes shining like a spooked pony. "Uuunnnhh," she grunted, kicking. The boat rocked from side to side. I sat on her legs, leaned into her face, and cupped my ear.

"What's that Mama? You say you're sorry you smacked me?"

"EeEe," came from behind the gag.

"You know, I've always hated that name. Dede. Sounds like a stutter. I might just change it. What do you think about Rita?"

Tears dribbled from her eyes and soaked the edges of the rag. "Eeees," she said.

"You're saying please? Speak up, Mama. I can't understand a word you're saying. Didn't you teach me not to mumble?" This made me laugh so hard I got the hiccups. "Can't understand," I gasped, after catching my breath.

"I know," I said. "Let's play a game. Remember when you took my knife for a week 'cause I was playing mumblety-peg and you said it was dangerous? And I told you I was really good at it?"

I rested the blade tip gently on the top of my left hand and held the handle in my right. With a quick flip of the wrist the knife spun toward Mama and buried itself in her stomach. She let out an "oof" and moaned.

I pulled the blade out and pointed it at her. "That wasn't an accident. It landed exactly where I wanted it to." I flipped the knife into the air and caught it by the handle. "Told you I was good."

I had a few more turns at the game, flipping the knife off my elbow, my finger, my chin, and even my nose. It made a kind of whizzing sound in the air, followed by a wet thump when it landed. Blood oozed from stabs in her chest, her arm, her thigh, and a couple more places. After a while she stopped moving and moaning and just stared at me.

I got bored with mumblety-peg, so I buried the knife deep in her belly, right where it had gone in the first time. I yanked up, making an opening big enough to stick my hand in.

"Ooh, nice and warm and slimy. Feels kinda neat, Mama. If you'd followed in Rita's footsteps, you could have been teaching me all along." I snickered. "Wait, I guess you are teaching me."

I took my time exploring, cutting here and there. People's intestines are blue just like critters. And smell just as bad when you cut into them. I finally got tired of Mama staring at me, so I drove the blade into her left eye.

Next came the hard part. I pulled out the knife, flipped the blade toward my stomach, and took a deep breath.

⌑⌑◈⌑⌑

The rowboat was bumping up against the shore when the hunter found us. He sucked in his breath and said, "Jesus Christ," in a shaky voice. I kept my eyes shut but let out a low moan, which wasn't too hard. Even shallow cuts hurt. Mama was way past moaning. He stumbled into the water and scooped me out of the boat. I screamed when he touched me, and he almost dropped me. While he struggled to hang onto me, I slipped Daddy's bloody fishing knife into the side pocket of his cargo pants. He laid me on the shore, and I screamed again. I wouldn't let him near me. After a while, another man ran up to us and I scooted away from the hunter, crying and pointing.

"Keep him away from me!"

My savior's name was Mike, Mike Tompkins. Or is it Thompson? Never can remember. And he really did save me. Oh, I wouldn't have died from the stab wounds. But, thanks to him, I left the hospital and went home to Daddy, a lucky survivor of a horrible crime. Mike, he's serving a life sentence for murder and attempted murder. My heartbreaking testimony and grief over my murdered mother convinced the jury.

How did I know the hunter would come along? I didn't.

That, I truly believe, was Rita looking out for me.

FISH COURSE - MERMAIDS & PIRATES

Recommended Wine: Pinot Grigio

Salt Pork

Eight strong sailors pulled on the oars of the longboat until it bumped gently against the hull of the four-masted barque, *Phoenix*. Heavily laden with plunder from the scuttled merchant ship, *Margate,* the boat rode low in the water. Three crewmen hoisted crates, sacks, and barrels upward to their mates aboard ship.

"To the hold," directed Quartermaster Cameron. A line of sailors snaked across the deck, carrying the booty down a steep, narrow ladder into the bowels of the ship.

Cameron followed the sailors into the hold, then dismissed them and began an inventory of the goods. Heavy footsteps soon interrupted his task. He whirled and bit back a curse when he saw the towering figure of Captain Vane.

"Mister Cameron." The captain crowded into the small space and ran his three-fingered left hand along the tops of the containers.

"Sir?"

Vane was an illiterate bully but a fearless leader in battle. The educated Cameron was well-qualified for the quartermaster role and ran the ship on a day-to-day basis. The captain's nickname among the sailors was "Weathervane" since his moods could spin as swiftly.

"A fine day's work," said Vane. He eyed Cameron. "And you will keep it secure?"

"Aye, Captain." Cameron had yet to find the culprit who had been stealing extra rations. "I'll stand guard myself if I must."

"Good, good." Vane picked up a jingling cloth pouch and lifted the lid of a small wooden chest. He smiled at the contents, then closed the lid and tucked the chest under his free arm. "I'll be taking these," he said, "just to be safe."

"Aye, Captain."

Cameron hadn't counted any of the coins or assessed the jewels yet. He was certain there would be less of both to be divided among the men at the end of the voyage. Sighing, he returned to his inventory, prying tops off crates, noting their contents, and then hammering them closed. Shipping containers were used and reused until they fell apart, so what was written on the outside seldom matched what was held within. After reading the words on the outside of the last hogshead, he pried its lid free. A fishy smell assailed his nostrils. Silvery scales floated in brine, gleaming in the dim light of the lantern.

"Hmmph. Salt pork, eh?"

He reached in, grabbed the fish with both hands, and pulled out a large tail, half again as tall as he was. Dropping it to the deck, he peered into the barrel and plunged his arm into the salty liquid as far as it would go. His fingers became entangled in copious amounts of long, thin strands. Seaweed? A young woman's face, eyes closed, emerged from the brine. What he had assumed to have been seaweed was in fact her long, dark hair. He thrust his other arm under her shoulders and pulled her from the barrel. Cameron lay the dripping body gently on the deck and stared in disbelief. She was perfectly preserved and quite beautiful. Also quite naked. To his shame and horror, he felt his loins stir. A gasp sounded at the entrance to the hold.

"What is *that* Mister Cameron?" The cook, Daniel, gaped at sight of the dead woman and the large lower half of a fish lying next to each other. His eyes flitted between the two. "Did she come apart?"

Cameron quickly stepped in front of the woman. "Come apart?"

"Surely she's a mermaid." Daniel pointed. "There's her tail!"

"Don't be ridiculous," snapped Cameron. "She's got legs."

Daniel examined the lower half of the fish. "Her legs would fit in 'ere."

After enlisting the cook's help in returning the woman to her watery tomb, he suggested that Daniel prepare the fish for the evening meal. The man gave him a horrified look and refused. "I ain't no cannibal, sir!" Cameron slid the fish back into the barrel.

He swore Daniel to secrecy, but there are no secrets aboard ship. The story of the beautiful mermaid found in a hogshead spread like wildfire. It didn't take long for Captain Vane to make his way back down to the hold.

"What's this I hear about a mermaid, Mister Cameron?"

The quartermaster shook his head wearily. "No, Captain. Not a mermaid. Just an unfortunate young lass. I don't know how she died or why she was in the barrel with the fish. And the merchants claim *we* are savages."

"Let's have a look then."

Cameron reluctantly pried the lid off the hogshead and lifted the woman until the captain could see her face.

"And the rest."

Cameron lifted her out completely and held her in his arms. The captain came closer, his greedy eyes running up and down her poor exposed body.

"Quite the beauty, isn't she?" Vane reached out and tweaked a nipple. "No wonder Daniel was so taken with her."

Cameron swiveled away to remove the girl from the captain's reach. "I'll just put her back," he said, his steady voice hiding the depth of his rage.

Stuart Cameron had been raised in Edinburgh by his widowed mother, surrounded by five sisters who all doted on him. This ill-fated stranger reminded him very much of them. He hammered the lid down and faced the captain, determined to protect her.

"We should try to find her family," he suggested. "She has all her teeth and shows no signs of hard work. She's probably wealthy. Her return might pay a considerable sum."

The captain stroked his beard. "Yes, you may be right. We can inquire discreetly at the next port." He waved his hand toward the hogshead. "Make sure no harm comes to her." He paused. "Not that she'd know." Vane strode away, chuckling to himself.

Cameron had already slung his hammock in the hold to protect the ship's stores. But now there was a greater need for his presence. Every crew member made a pilgrimage (some more than one) to the hold and begged to see the mermaid, only to be turned away. The cook made matters worse by exaggerating his encounter, so that she became more beautiful with each telling of the story.

Cameron sewed a shroud from scraps of sailcloth for Katherine, as he thought of her—for she deserved a name. The shroud would cover her nakedness and provide some protection from the more licentious members of the crew, and from Captain Vane in particular. He waited until the only men awake were the sailors on watch before prying the lid from the barrel.

He lifted Katherine from the brine and placed her gently in his hammock. Water dripped from her hair as she swayed with the motion of the ship. Cameron spread the shroud on the deck and turned to lift her. He paused and gazed at her face, just for a moment, before sealing her in the protective shroud. She looked as if she were merely sleeping. He stroked her cheek, her fine nose, her strong chin, brushing away dried grains of salt. Her skin was cool, but pliant. What color were her eyes?

"What happened to you?" he asked. "How did you come to such a sad ending?"

He touched her lips, slightly less full than when he discovered her yesterday. The salt was drawing moisture from her body. Her beauty wouldn't last much longer. He leaned over and gently kissed her mouth, tasting salt, but something else as well—a sweetness, like honey. He kissed her again, sliding his tongue between her lips. Her nectar coated his tongue and made him gasp. His vision blurred until all he could see was the beauty in front of him.

Cameron ran his hand down her slender neck, hesitated, then cupped her breast. It just filled his hand.

"Did nobody love you?" he asked his silent companion.

The poor girl deserved to be loved. Driven by a force he could not resist, he moved as if in a dream, peeling off his shirt and breeches until he stood naked before her.

"Now we are equal," he told her.

He leaned over the swaying hammock for another sweet kiss. Her hair caressed his crotch and he stiffened. But he felt no shame. His excitement was the highest compliment, the last compliment Katherine would ever receive. He slid into the hammock and pressed his naked body against hers. Her body seemed to warm in his embrace. He buried his nose in her hair and inhaled deeply. He picked up her hand and kissed the palm, then sucked on each salty finger. Surrounding her wet hand with his, he pushed it toward his erection, closed her fingers, then moaned as he almost immediately ejaculated. The release snapped him out of his trance. He scrambled from the hammock, nearly throwing Katherine to the deck in his haste.

"I'm sorry, I'm so sorry," he gasped. The sweetness from her kisses gone suddenly bitter, he gagged and spat.

He'd just stepped into his breeches when a cough sounded at the entryway to the hold. There stood Vane, with an ugly grin on his face.

"What do we have here, Mister Cameron? Not so high and mighty now, are you?" The captain reached for his belt buckle and stepped toward the hammock. "I'm sure the filly would prefer a more skilled rider."

Cameron put his head down and charged like an angry bull, striking Vane in the stomach and driving the breath out of him. The captain crashed against a stack of crates, scrabbling for his sheathed dagger. But the quartermaster was quicker and disarmed him. He had no idea how long

Vane had been watching or how much he'd seen, but word of his indiscretion could not be allowed to spread. He drove the dagger into the captain's throat.

He had little time before someone investigated the noise. He swept Katherine from the hammock and plunged her back into the hogshead, leaving the upper half of her body draped over the edge and hiding the lower. Next, he unbuckled Vane's belt and pulled his breeches off. He dragged the body close to the barrel and cried out for help. Sailors pounded down the ladder to find that their Captain had tried to fuck the mermaid, had been caught, and had attacked Mister Cameron.

Vane's body was sewn into the shroud intended for Katherine. The next morning, the crew removed their caps and bowed their heads as their late Captain slid into the sea. The all-hands meeting following the burial resulted in Cameron being voted captain, which he declined. He suggested the first mate, Mister Owens, in his stead. The man was a fine tactician with a steady disposition, popular among the men.

But throughout the course of the day, the mood of the crew darkened. They went from fascination with the mermaid to certainty that she had brought bad luck to the ship. No one had yet approached Captain Owens, but it was just a matter of time.

Cameron returned to the hold that evening, placed his crossed arms on the hogshead and leaned his head on them. "I can't protect you, Katherine," he whispered.

"From anyone. Please forgive me for what I must do." He straightened and went in search of the cook.

At dawn, Cameron once more gathered the crew on deck. He drew back a rough blanket covering an object at his feet. There lay the mermaid in her natural form. From the waist down, her body took the form of a large fish. Only Cameron and Daniel were close enough to see the fine stitches securing the tail to her body. The rest of the men stood slack-jawed, finally allowed a full view of her, naked from the waist up.

Cameron cleared the lump from his throat with a cough and stood tall. "This creature can no longer stay aboard," he said in a booming voice. "She has brought bickering and bad luck to the *Phoenix*." He nodded to the cook, who bent to pick up the tail. Cameron slid his hands under her shoulders, and they moved to the side of the ship. With a splash, the mermaid was returned to the sea.

Even after ridding the ship of the mermaid, the sailors blamed her for any small bit of bad luck they encountered, from a torn sail to a twisted ankle. It took both Mister Cameron and Captain Owens to calm their fears. The cook was particularly rattled and came to see Cameron in his quarters.

"She were really a mermaid, weren't she, sir?" He twisted his cap in his hands, "You saw how her legs fit into the tail so neat."

"But we sewed her in, Daniel," Cameron said gently.

"Aye, we did, sir. And I'll never speak of that to anyone. But she were a mermaid what had been torn apart by someone on the *Margate*." He spat on the deck. "Savages!"

The two days Katherine had been aboard seemed like a dream to Cameron. A dream that had turned into a nightmare. There was no harm, and much benefit, in letting Daniel think she had been a real mermaid.

He draped his arm around the cook's shoulders. "Yes, Daniel. A mermaid, she was. And now she and her curse are gone. You have nothing to fear."

The man seemed satisfied and was noticeably cheerier in the following days. The crew settled back into their routine. Captain Owens set a course for a busy shipping channel where he could take his pick of targets. The *Phoenix* was speeding along when she caught a backing wind, signaling bad weather ahead. A storm was upon them swiftly with darkening skies and rising seas.

Cameron was below when the storm struck and struggled to reach the main deck as the ship was tossed about. He climbed the ladder to a fearsome sight—a wall of black water on one side of the ship and a deep trench on the other. He lashed himself to the base of the ratlines and held on for dear life. The giant wave crashed down on the ship and he watched helplessly as sailors who'd not been so quick were swept overboard. The main mast snapped and plunged to the deck, crushing an unlucky sailor. A hole gaped in the hull, swallowing water from each great wave, pushing the ship lower until the main deck was only feet above the roiling ocean.

Cameron looked toward the unmanned, wildly spinning wheel and unlashed himself from the ratlines. He worked his way forward, clinging to everything that was secured. Lashing himself to the base of the wheel, he stopped its spinning and squinted through the driving rain for other survivors, finally spotting a man with his arms clenched around a cannon as if it were his lover.

"Ahoy," he shouted.

The man looked up with desperation in his eyes—Daniel, the cook. They were the only two sailors still aboard. Anyone who'd been below had surely drowned and all above had been swept from the deck. A loud crack opened another hole in the hull. A churning trough of water raged between the two men.

"Jump!" Cameron urged. "Get clear before she goes down!"

Daniel shook his head and clung tighter to the cannon. But when the ship splintered behind him, he had no choice. He quickly crossed himself, jumped from the disintegrating ship, and disappeared into the boiling blackness.

Cameron held the useless wheel steady. The rudder gone, what remained of the hull nearly full of water, there was nothing more to do. He cut the line holding him to the wheel and joined Daniel in the roiling seas.

He allowed himself to sink, then swam strongly underwater away from the remains of the ship. Once it went down, he could circle back for wreckage to cling to. A pale figure floated upright in the dark water. Daniel? He swam faster in hope of saving the man. But it was not a man. Katherine! No, not Katherine. But a live mermaid, a beautiful, smiling creature. She approached and wrapped him in her arms. He could do nothing but stare into her deep green eyes, lungs bursting for air.

"Thank you, Stuart." A lilting voice sounded in his head. "You did your best for our sister."

The creature cupped the back of his head and drew him in for a kiss. He tasted the familiar, intoxicating sweetness of her lips, then opened his mouth and allowed the ocean to pour in.

SILENT MAIDENS

Daniel remembered little of his rescue from the angry seas. He'd floated, draped over a large piece of the deck, for more than a day. A passing merchant ship plucked him from the waters near Hispaniola and carried him to its next port in the Bahamas. He was delirious with fever most of the way and his rescuers took him to the local hospital. When his fever broke, he opened his eyes to see a constable seated at his bedside.

"Morning, Mister Wold," said the constable. "You're a very lucky man. I have a few questions for you if you're up to it." Before Daniel could object, the constable continued. "What ship were you on and what were the circumstances of its loss?"

Daniel's heart raced. "It, it were the *Phoenix*, sir," he stammered. "But I was pressed on as cook. I couldn't escape, sir. They would have killed me."

The constable raised his eyebrows. "Pressed, eh?"

"Yes, sir. As God is my witness, sir."

The penalty for piracy was hanging. Daniel did not intend to escape a watery death only to end up dancing at the end of a rope. After a long stare, the constable nodded and dipped a quill into an inkwell. He looked up, quill poised over a leatherbound book lying open on a small table.

"Lucky for you, there's no one left to say otherwise. Now, tell me how the ship went down."

Relieved at having gotten away with the lie, Daniel proceeded to tell the truth—the *Phoenix* was cursed. She had taken aboard a dead mermaid hidden in a hogshead pillaged from the merchant ship, *Margate*. Within two days, the captain was killed in a fight with the quartermaster and the mermaid had been returned to the sea. But it was too late. One week after ridding herself of the unlucky creature, the *Phoenix* had run into a huge storm which tore the sturdy ship apart.

At the first mention of the mermaid, the constable's eyebrows rose again. By the time Daniel finished his tale, the man's eyebrows had completely vanished under the brim of his helmet.

"Sailors believe in omens," the constable said slowly. "I can't understand it myself, but I'm no sailor." He blotted the book and closed it carefully. "If I were you, I'd take the fact that you are still alive as a very lucky omen, and not return to sea."

"Never again, sir," said Daniel.

Once out of the hospital, Daniel found work at The Silent Maiden, a tavern near the waterfront. His cooking skills and experience dealing with drunken and rowdy men served him well. But the nearness of beer, mead, and whisky did not. When in his cups, he regaled the patrons with stories of the beautiful dead mermaid and how she had enraptured all the men aboard. These stories earned him the reputation of being slightly mad, but harmless. Most acknowledged the existence of mermaids, but few claimed to have actually seen them, and assumed that Daniel's brush with death had addled his brains.

But even in his most drunken state, Daniel told no one of his last sight of Quartermaster Cameron. After plunging from the deck of the sinking ship, he had opened his eyes and swum desperately toward the surface. He spied Cameron in the water a few feet away in the embrace of a mermaid—a live mermaid. Cameron returned the embrace, gently stroking the creature's dark hair as the entwined pair spiraled slowly down into darkness.

Daniel had been working at The Silent Maiden for a month when a man arrived and insisted on speaking to him. The stranger waited for two hours and three pints of beer until Daniel finished in the kitchen.

"Mister Wold?" The man stood and offered his hand. "Tom Smith, late of the *Falmouth*."

Daniel shook the proffered hand. "The *Falmouth*, eh. You are a lucky man, sir."

"As are you. I understand you was aboard the *Phoenix*." Smith tilted his mug to drain the last of the beer and thumped it onto the rough wooden table. "That cursed ship yet exists."

Daniel sat, his knees suddenly wobbly. "What do you mean?"

"The *Falmouth* did not founder on its own."

Daniel held up a hand and signaled the serving wench to bring two more mugs of beer. "Tell me what happened."

Smith took a long swallow and began. "After a clear day, it were evening when the lookout spied another ship. She sailed toward us with great speed. Not natural if you ask me." He took another swallow while Daniel nodded encouragement. "When the lookout cried the name of the ship, nobody believed it. The *Phoenix* was long gone. But this ship kept coming and the captain ordered full sails. She looked like a pirate ship and we was heavily laden. We couldn't outrun her. She pulled alongside and I spied a man behind the wheel, laughing."

"What did this man look like?"

"Very tall with ginger hair. And a yellow greatcoat. There was no other sailors aboard. Then I saw her."

"Her?"

"The mermaid. She clung to the bowsprit like a live figurehead."

"Are you sure it wasn't the figurehead?"

Smith shook his head emphatically. "Sure as I'm sitting 'ere. She turned her head and smiled at me." His eyes glazed over and he took on a dreamy look. "So beautiful."

"And dangerous!" Daniel slammed his mug down, startling the man back to the present. "Go on."

"The pirate ship ran side by side until they forced us against the rocks, where the *Falmouth* broke up. But," Smith looked directly at Daniel, his eyes wide, "the *Phoenix* disappeared as soon as we hit. I were thrown to the deck and when I picked m'self up, she were gone." He held his hand up. "I swear it." He leaned forward. "Tell me true, sir. Do you believe me?"

Daniel sighed. "Call me Daniel and I'll call you Tom. After what we've both been through, we should be mates. Aye, Tom. I believe you."

The description of the man piloting the pirate ship matched Mister Cameron perfectly. Somehow, the *Phoenix* had lived up to her name, rising not from the ashes but from the depths to sail again. And she brought with her a ghostly Cameron and his new paramour.

Matthew Dalrymple, the local Director of Higgins Shipping Company, was the next visitor to seek Daniel out at the tavern. Dalrymple was a foppish man, attired in a velvet waistcoat and a feathered tricorn hat. He brushed off the rough wooden bench with his handkerchief before sitting down.

"I understand you've heard Smith's story," Dalrymple began without preamble.

"Yes, sir. I have."

"I believe Smith was influenced by your tale and his chattering has spooked my other crews. And since you're the one who started this ridiculous mermaid story, I'd like you to help me end it."

Daniel shot to his feet. "I am no liar, sir! The *Margate* carried a dead mermaid. I saw it with me own eyes."

"Fine, fine. I apologize." Dalrymple waved his hand limply, urging Daniel back into his seat. "You are aware that both the *Margate* and the *Falmouth* were Higgins Company ships," he stated.

"No, I wasn't," said Daniel slowly.

"My crews are fearful. But if you were to join the crew of one of our ships, just for one sailing, it would reassure them that they are in no danger from the *Phoenix*. I will pay you handsomely," he added, naming a sum unimaginable to Daniel.

"The sea only gives a man so many chances, sir, and I believe I've used all of mine."

"I'll double the amount."

Daniel hesitated. With the money earned, he could open his own tavern. He did miss being at sea. And if they spotted the *Phoenix,* surely Cameron would recognize him and do him no harm. The possibility of seeing the live mermaid again was intriguing.

"Just one sailing," Daniel agreed.

The *Portsmouth* was scheduled to sail in two weeks. Daniel helped select and load the food stores. He would be assistant to the cook. The rest of the crew seemed in awe of him, eager to engage him in conversation about the *Phoenix,* its famed quartermaster, and of course, the mermaid.

Before the *Portsmouth* sailed, the ghostly pirate ship was spotted once more, by an East India Company ship, the *Rooster.* The *Phoenix* approached rapidly and sailed alongside for a while. Many of the crew reported seeing the mermaid on the bowsprit. Then the pilot of the *Phoenix* gave a jaunty wave and turned away, vanishing into the horizon.

The safe passage of the *Rooster,* combined with Daniel's presence, lent confidence to the crew of the *Portsmouth.* The merchant ship sailed from Nassau on a clear day, loaded with sugar and rum to take back to England. Daniel pushed down his niggling doubts and enjoyed the high spirits and camaraderie of his fellow sailors.

Daniel's hopeful outlook blew away like foam from a whitecap on the sixth day at sea. The lookout spied a ship in the distance. The *Phoenix* was upon them in an impossibly short time. He stood next to the rail and stared at his former shipmate, who looked as real and solid as any of the *Portsmouth's* sailors. His gaze moved to the bowsprit. The same mermaid who'd lured Cameron into the depths perched there. Her eyes pulled at him, as deep green as the ocean they traveled. A shout drew his attention back to Cameron.

"Daniel! Welcome," the ghost said.

The cook felt the tug of the mermaid, urging him to look at her again. He shook his head and stared hard at Cameron.

"Mister Cameron," he answered. "We mean you no harm. Let us pass."

"Ah, that I cannot do. I have no quarrel with you, my friend." He nodded his head toward the mermaid. "She's the one you must convince."

Daniel glanced back toward the mermaid. A musical voice sounded in his head. "Join us, Daniel." He clenched his eyes shut and clapped both hands over his ears.

The panicked first mate clutched at his arm, shouting, "Mister Wold, make them go away!"

Daniel started and tore his arm from the man's grasp. When he opened his eyes, the mermaid captured him in her emerald gaze once more. Try as he might, he was helpless to look away.

"Help us seek justice for our sister," she sang.

He had worked so hard to escape the sea, but the dream of owning a tavern now seemed petty. Surely the sea was where he belonged. This beautiful creature would keep him safe. Relief washed over him when he stopped resisting. He hummed along with her song and smiled as he clambered over the rail and plunged into the water.

The *Phoenix* sped away from the shattered remains of the *Portsmouth*. Before it disappeared, surviving sailors say they saw two men aboard, standing side by side—the ginger-haired pilot and the ship's former cook. The mermaid rode the bowsprit, urging the ghost ship onward.

MEAT COURSE -
CREATURES GREAT & SMALL

Recommended Wine: Cabernet Sauvignon

THE WAGES OF SIN

July 14, 1975

Yevgeny Petrovitch grunted as he pulled the heavily laden cart over the uneven forest path. Only another half kilometer to go. He'd selected the remote location of his garden plot out of extreme caution. The newly developed fertilizer, stolen from his employer, had been deemed a failure when applied to pine and spruce trees. But Yevgeny had noticed its effectiveness on smaller shrubs and bushes and had smuggled the remaining mixture out, rather than dispose of it as ordered. After four trips over the past week, this was the last load.

It would be perfect for his special crop.

He mixed the fertilizer with compost and shoveled it onto the base of his marijuana plants, disappearing into the towering rows as he worked. When finished, he walked the perimeter of the plot, inspecting the wire fencing he'd put up to keep deer from destroying his yield. Birdsong and the rustling of leaves filled the air. He breathed in the spicy smell of his crop and smiled. Satisfied that all was well, he whistled as he began the three-kilometer walk home.

The huge Carpathian wild boar traveled alone. Only during mating season did he seek out others of his kind; females to mate with, males to fight. His days were a constant search for food to maintain his bulk.

His keen nose led him to a patch of tall, spiky-leaved plants enclosed by a shiny barrier. He tore off a mouthful of overhanging leaves and munched. When no more tender leaves were within reach, he lowered his head to the barrier, hooked it with his tusks, and tore it aside. A musty, delicious smell came from the earth at the base of the plants. He snuffled and dug his tusks into the dirt, gobbling mouthfuls of the rich dark soil and rolling it over his tongue in search of earthworms. After eating his fill, he felt sleepy and retired to a nearby small cave to rest.

The boar returned to the patch the next day, and the next. Each morning he awoke to find he'd outgrown his nighttime resting place. Familiar paths through the forest became too narrow, so he leaned his great shoulders against the trees to widen the way. His head brushed the canopy of the forest and at times he could even see over the tops of the trees. His increased size required more food. A lot more food.

After wiping out the patch of spiky plants, he began stripping leaves from trees, often pulling them down in his frenzy. He drove his tusks into the earth in search of insects, toppling even more trees. His taste for meat increased. Small mammals were mere snacks. Anything living became potential prey. He discovered that his nemesis, the gray wolf, made a fine meal and since wolves traveled in a pack, he could kill three or four at a time.

July 21, 1975

Yevgeny gaped in horror at the remains of his crop. He hadn't been to the plot since he'd added the last of the fertilizer, not wanting to attract attention by visiting too often. His feet sunk into the soil, as soft as if it had been freshly turned. He approached the flattened fence, searching for signs of who or what could have done this. An enormous print in the mud caught his eye—a cloven hoof, two meters long and a meter wide. He crossed himself and murmured a quick prayer before hurrying home, glancing nervously over his shoulder the whole way. He must speak to Father Kozlov.

The devil himself had come to Onega.

July 24, 1975

Father Kozlov followed Yevgeny to the destroyed garden and viewed the giant hoofprint for himself. He scoured the area and discovered more prints, enough to ascertain that they had been made by a four-legged animal, not a two-legged devil. But what creature could make prints of that size? Poor Yevgeny looked like he would have preferred the devil, and Father Kozlov almost agreed with him.

He reported the giant hoofprints to the mayor, only to be met with disdain. Not surprising; it was difficult to believe even having seen the proof. Kozlov also told his army reserve unit. Most of them were avid hunters who theorized that the prints belonged to a new species of boar. Eager to acquire the ultimate trophy kill, they spent the next few days gathering an arsenal of heavy weaponry in preparation for the hunt.

July 31, 1975

The boar stood on a hill at the edge of the forest, gazing down upon a warren of humans. He'd always avoided people, but he was so, so hungry.

He broke into a trot and charged down the incline, shaking the ground with every step. He shook his massive head, sending ropes of saliva flying from his tusks to land on the ground like giant slugs. Two people ran screaming just ahead of him, one of them carrying a smaller human. He snatched them up and crushed them in his mouth, enjoying the burst of blood and crunch of bone.

The boar slowed to a walk as he surveyed the area for more food. A patch of greenery among the stone structures beckoned. He strode toward it, his giant hooves crushing everything and everyone in his path. He heard popping noises and felt a barrage of stings on his haunches, but his thick, bristled skin and layers of fat protected him.

A chorus of sounds to his rear increased in volume. His massive neck prevented him from swiveling his head, so he turned his body sideways to see his pursuers. Flames exploded from near a huddled group of humans, and a long, pointed thing hurtled toward his flank. The boar roared as the object tore through his unguarded belly. Loops of bloody, glistening innards dangled from his wound as he spun to escape the pain. The boar faced the humans, his enormous chest and shoulders his best defense. He bellowed, lowered his head, and galloped toward them. All scattered but one.

Father Kozlov knelt in front of a grenade launcher, trembling as he watched the giant animal advance. The beast must be over nine meters in height! A sudden rush of adrenaline calmed his nerves and brought his sharpshooter training into focus. He steadied the sight of the launcher, aiming at the giant left eye. Waiting until the boar was nearly upon him, he squeezed the trigger and turned to run. The grenade exploded, hurling chunks of bone and blobs of brain matter everywhere. The priest was knocked to the ground by a flying piece of skull. The massive animal collapsed on top of him, delivering Father Kozlov into the arms of God.

—◦◆◦—

The townspeople worked frantically to move the great beast off the body of their savior. It took fifty men and two hours to dismember the boar. A solemn procession formed to carry Kozlov's crushed body to the church. The remains of the boar were left until the next day, when they would be burned in a large pit.

During the night, a pack of gray wolves slunk into town, lured by the familiar scent of their favorite prey. The alpha male led the pack toward the mound of boar meat, and they ate their fill before tearing off chunks to carry back to the den for their pups.

August 2, 1975

Yevgeny wept at the funeral of the heroic priest. He'd watched, frozen in fear, as the brave soldiers battled the beast. After the boar was slain, cowardice stilled his tongue and prevented him from confessing that he had, in fact, created the freakish monster by applying the stolen fertilizer to his illegal crop. If the townspeople found out, the best he could hope for was a quick hanging. But those who lost loved ones wouldn't settle for such a merciful end.

—◦◆◦—

Knowing how difficult the funeral had been, Marushka served her husband's favorite meal that night, borscht with black bread. Afterward Yevgeny leaned back, hands laced over his full stomach, and let out a satisfied belch. Even their usually fussy young son, Mikhail, had finished the meal, mopping up the borscht with chunks of bread in an imitation of his father.

Marushka beamed at her husband. "You like?"

"Excellent! Did you use different spices?"

"Not exactly. The new harvest of beets. They are so big and tasty, I barely needed to season the borscht at all!"

Yevgeny's lungs seized. He pushed back from the table, knocking his chair to the floor, and rushed from the house. *No, no! It couldn't be! There had only been one small bag left and he'd hidden it beneath a tarp!* He slid to a stop at the garden shed and braced himself against the doorway, panting. The fertilizer bag lay on its side, empty and crumpled.

Yevgeny staggered into the yard and spewed a stream of crimson borscht at the feet of his puzzled wife. He bent over, hands on knees, trying not to black out. An eerie sound pierced his veil of self-pity and misery. He raised his head and listened.

A chorus of wolves keened in the distance. Their howls sounded stronger than usual...more demanding, almost frenzied. And much, much hungrier.

A MISCHIEF IN GORDONSVILLE

The small grey creature balanced on its hind legs, stretching toward the morsel of stale bread just above its head. It reached with tiny pink forefeet, extending the toes like small human hands. Finally, it leaned back on its haunches and leapt straight up, snatching the prize from the fingers of Sergeant Beau Amberson.

"Well done," he chuckled, watching the rat stuff the bread past its long yellow incisors.

A door opened behind him, releasing a babble of noise from the crowded hospital ward. Amberson's heart accelerated and he spun toward the doorway, blocking the view of the rat's hairless tail as it disappeared through a small opening in the wall.

"Oh. Sergeant Amberson. You gave me quite a start!" The matron of the Gordonsville Receiving Hospital stood in the narrow doorway of the storage room, hand to her chest.

"Just getting fresh bandages, Mrs. Millett." He gestured at the shelves piled with linen.

"With the door closed?"

He shrugged. "Must've swung shut."

Abigail Millett frowned. "Sergeant, I do appreciate your assistance, but remember that you must work with the staff. Next time, ask someone to retrieve supplies for you."

"But they were all busy. And Corporal Winston's wound has soaked through." He dropped his gaze. "I was only trying to help."

She patted his shoulder. "I know, my boy. We are all doing our best." Picking up a handful of clean rags, she led him out of the room, but not before hesitating in the doorway and sniffing the air.

Amberson exhaled slowly as he shut the door to the storage room. The stench of urine was becoming stronger. He'd need to find another location within the hospital to meet with his friend.

Sergeant Amberson had fought valiantly at Chancellorsville under General Stonewall Jackson for three days before the general was wounded. Along with most men in his company, Amberson was fiercely loyal to General Jackson and the injury of his commander had shaken him.

Two days after Jackson was wounded, Amberson took a musket ball in his left forearm, just missing the elbow. However, he continued to fight one-armed until a cannonball landed nearby, knocking him unconscious. He remembered little of the transport from battlefield to hospital. When he awoke from surgery to remove the ball from his arm, the doctor told him how lucky he was. He could have lost the limb, as did his beloved commander. Two weeks after his surgery, Amberson heard that General Jackson had succumbed to his injuries. The dreadful news released the guilt he'd been holding at bay, overwhelming him and sending him into a deep depression.

The Gordonsville Receiving Hospital, like many near the front lines of the war, was severely understaffed. With consent from the doctors, Mrs. Millett recruited soldiers who were on the road to recovery to help care for those more seriously wounded. Amberson believed that keeping busy would help him escape the jaws of the black dog of depression, so he agreed to help. With little training and sketchy supervision, Amberson joined the ranks of soldier/orderly three months after his arrival.

Amberson's new role allowed him to roam the hospital at will. Situated next to the railroad tracks, the building had been The Exchange Hotel before the war. Its faded elegance still shone through, even when the bedrooms, parlors, and both large outside porches were filled with wounded men. He took advantage of his newfound freedom and explored all three stories of the great building.

He'd been poking around the storage room off the second-floor ward late one evening, familiarizing himself with its contents, when a scratching, scuttling noise came from the corner. He glanced over to see a large rat sitting on its haunches with front paws folded over its belly, like a man after a particularly satisfying meal. The creature regarded him with strange, pale blue eyes.

Rats, a constant presence in the hospital, ate anything they could, including poultices still applied to a soldier's body. Mrs. Millett was in a perpetual state of war with the pests. Amberson, however, had kept a pet rat when he was a boy and found them highly intelligent.

Intrigued by this unusual specimen, he crouched and held out his hand. The rat dropped to all fours, whiskers twitching, and maintained eye contact. Amberson chirruped and the rat squeaked in reply but kept its distance. Slowly, Amberson reached into his pocket and pulled out a small piece of hardtack. He held it off to the side and the rat followed the food with its eyes. Amberson tossed the scrap toward the rat, which grabbed it and disappeared through a hole at the base of the wall.

Amberson returned to the storage room the following night. Finding it empty, he was about to leave when he heard the familiar scuttling and turned to see the rat once again perched on its haunches watching him with a cool blue gaze that seemed oddly familiar. This time, Amberson waited until the rat had taken a couple of steps toward him before delivering the treat. The rat ran off with its bounty, but not before uttering a series of squeaks, as if it were saying thank you.

Over the next few weeks, Amberson and the rat became companions. He volunteered to set Mrs. Millett's traps in the areas his friend frequented, but then neglected to bait them. The animal appeared grateful for the intervention and even brought some of its brethren to visit on occasion.

Since his arrival at the hospital Amberson had been plagued by insomnia and, when he did sleep, was haunted by vivid nightmares of battle. Particularly of Chancellorsville. One night, he bolted upright in his cot drenched in sweat. The rat had the same light blue eyes as the great Stonewall Jackson! It was highly intelligent, more so than any other rat he'd ever encountered, and its posture at times was almost human. Could it be? Was it possible?

He slipped out of bed and crept from closet to closet before finding the rat in the pantry. The rat paused its scavenging and looked up, its blue eyes reflecting the dim light of the moon streaming through the single high window.

"General?" Amberson felt both foolish and hopeful.

The rat bobbed its head and squeezed through a hole in the wall.

A shaken Amberson returned to his cot, memories of the General spinning through his mind. Had the rat nodded in the affirmative? Or had he imagined it? Was he going mad?

The following week saw an influx of patients, so he had little time to pursue his theory. But after a lighter-than-usual day, he slipped from his cot and silently searched for the rat. Finding it once again in the pantry, he crouched and whispered, "General Jackson?"

The rat approached him, sat back on its haunches, and raised its left foreleg high in the air.

Overcome by sudden dizziness, Amberson clutched a shelf for balance. General Jackson had once had a habit of making just such a motion! In fact, he had been injured in the left hand at the First Battle of Bull Run while holding his arm high. Amberson crouched and cupped his hands. The rat stepped into them. He lifted the creature until they were eye to eye. Tears blurred Amberson's vision.

As a member of the 18th North Carolina Infantry, Sergeant Amberson was one of the sentries who'd been ordered to fire upon Jackson and his party as they returned to camp; a horrible case of mistaken identity. He had no way of knowing whether his bullet had led to the general's death.

The rat ground its teeth rapidly, a sign of contentment. Could this also be a gesture of forgiveness?

Amberson placed the creature back on the ground. It raised itself on its haunches, gave a final one-legged salute, and scuttled into the wall. The man dropped his face into his hands and sobbed.

Convinced that the rat was indeed his beloved general reborn, Amberson did everything he could to make up for possibly killing the man. First and foremost, he ensured the rat didn't want for food, setting aside bits of his own rations to feed the creature. When he came upon a rare slice of lemon, whatever niggling doubt may have remained as to the nature of his new friend was erased. Lemons had been a favorite of Jackson the man. Jackson the rat gobbled the lemon, then begged for more.

Once Amberson realized who he was dealing with, he no longer required Jackson to perform silly tricks and was embarrassed that he'd ever asked the great soul to do so. Jackson brought more and more rats with him on his visits, seemingly building his own personal mischief.

The soldier felt a responsibility to ensure that Jackson and his friends were well-fed. Acquiring that much "spare" food in a time of scarcity was challenging, but Amberson sought opportunities to glean more food.

He'd been successful until the day a large sack of dried hominy was left unattended in the kitchen. Glancing around, he set down the meal trays he'd been about to deliver and scooped a double handful of grain from the sack, filling both pockets. He then quickly sliced a slab of pork from the chopping block. He was about to pocket that as well when Mrs. Millett swept into the room.

"Pork is not on the menu until dinner, Sergeant. Are we not feeding you well enough?" She stood with her hands on her hips, blocking the doorway.

"Umm, it's for Private Sullivan, Ma'am." Amberson shuffled his feet, holding the pork in front of his body. "He had a very bad night and was begging for meat. I should have asked permission first, but he reminds me so of my brother." He gave her his best pleading look.

Unmoved, she shook her head. "Put it back. We must preserve our rations, and Private Sullivan will receive his meat tonight, along with the others. There can be no special treatment. Do you understand?"

Amberson returned the pork to the block, continuing to face the matron to better conceal the bulge of purloined grain in his pockets.

"I'm very disappointed in you, Sergeant. You should know better. Now, deliver those trays."

"I'm sorry, Ma'am. It won't happen again."

Amberson made sure it didn't. The matron never again caught him with stolen food. But his past success at feeding the mischief led to another problem. The hospital staff noticed the increased rat population, as did Mrs. Millett, who intensified her campaign against the pests.

After noting that the traps set by Amberson never caught any rats, she took the responsibility away from him and gave it to another orderly. The matron personally inspected all traps once they were set and had poison added to the bait in the event a rat managed to carry it away.

She went on a cleaning binge, assigning orderlies to move shelves and scrub everything in sight to eliminate places where the vermin could hide. Holes in walls and floors were flushed with water, then sealed off. Two weeks after she started her campaign, over two dozen rats had been trapped, poisoned, or clubbed to death.

It became harder for Amberson to meet with his friend as their rendezvous points were cleared of clutter and rat passageways through the building closed. He didn't see Jackson for the next three weeks, but neither (thankfully) had he found him among the casualties. The rat's skill at evading traps, unlike his followers, reinforced Amberson's belief in the animal's true nature.

One night after the latest losses to the colony, a doe and two pups, he felt a sharp pain on his ankle and threw back the blanket to see Jackson crouched at the foot of his cot. Blood trickled down Amberson's instep and smeared the rat's front teeth. The creature's blue eyes blazed, and he nodded his head vigorously but remained silent, as if aware of the danger of waking anyone else.

Amberson's emotions see-sawed—relief at seeing Jackson, shock at being bitten, and finally fear of being discovered. He scanned the dormitory in panic. The other orderlies were still asleep. He slipped on boots, scooped the rat into his blanket, and carried him outside to the gardening shed. By the light of the moon, he released Jackson onto the ground. The general glared and stamped his front feet.

"I'm sorry," Amberson whispered. "She's on a tear. I'm doing everything I can."

Jackson's noticeable weight loss showed the effect of Mrs. Millett's efforts. A skinny rat scurried out from the shed and stood beside him. Then another and another, a seething carpet of grey bodies. The rats were silent, beady eyes fixed on their general.

Amberson's jaw dropped. There must be nearly two hundred rats! He hadn't realized how large the mischief had grown.

Jackson stood on his haunches and raised his left front leg. After a rapid series of squeaks ending in a scream, he dropped to all fours and led his army past the vegetable garden toward the edge of the surrounding woods. Amberson followed at a distance. When the mass of rats made a sharp right turn, he realized where they were going and broke into a run.

He didn't catch up until they halted in front of two graves dug just that morning. Jackson perched on a mound of freshly turned earth and squeaked once more. The army of rats began digging. In no time they had uncovered the body of Private Massie, a boy of just seventeen, mortally wounded in his first engagement. The eyes were the first to go, then lips were nibbled and forced open to yield the tender tongue. A trio of rats joined forces to claw and chew through the belly, opening it for others to bury their pointed noses in bloody bowels.

Amberson stood frozen, sickened but afraid to sound the alarm. If he did, he would betray his general. He'd been given a second chance to serve the great soul. But the rats were desecrating a soldier's body! This boy didn't deserve such a fate after his heroic death. Overcoming his indecision, he jogged back to the gardening shed and returned with a shovel. He swung it toward the cluster of rats, scattering them. The shovel missed the rats but embedded itself in the chest of the corpse. Amberson let go of the handle and backed away, horrified. The shovel stood upright as if it had sprouted from the dead boy.

Amberson's legs gave out and he crumpled to the ground with a cold sweat trickling down his back. He clambered to his hands and knees and vomited, then crawled to a large oak, propped his back against it and closed his eyes. Exhausted, he didn't know how long he rested—he may even have slept. A soft squeak and the abrasive crunch of grinding teeth roused him. Jackson sat at his feet, belly round and distended, fur cleansed of blood and shining. His army was nowhere in sight.

"General," Amberson rasped through his scalded throat. "This could have been one of your men." He flailed his arm toward the pitiful remains. "You always looked out for your soldiers."

The rat nodded, lifted his left front leg, waddled away, then looked back over his shoulder before continuing.

Amberson wearily pushed himself to his feet and followed. Jackson led him to a clearing just beyond the cemetery. The clearing was filled with a pile of rats, bellies full and sound asleep. Jackson captured Amberson in his blue gaze, as if willing him to understand.

"*These* are your soldiers now," said Amberson, realization dawning. "But you cannot do this again." He crouched and cupped his hands. "I promise you'll have enough food. All of you."

Jackson crawled into the sergeant's cupped hands. Amberson lifted the creature to eye level, and a wordless understanding passed between them. The man placed the general gently on the pile, where he curled up to sleep with his soldiers.

Amberson returned to Massie's grave to rebury what was left of the private. He pried the shovel from the boy's chest and had no sooner filled his first shovelful of dirt when he heard a gasp. He whirled to see a horrified Mrs. Millett, clutching her dressing gown and pulling it close in the cold night air.

"What are you doing?" she cried.

"I, I can explain." Amberson stopped. How could he *possibly* explain? Surely he looked like some sort of ghoul or a graverobber. He tried again. "I couldn't sleep so I came to the pump for some water. I heard noises from the graveyard and came to investigate."

"Noises? What sort of noises?"

Amberson stepped toward the matron. She pulled a small pistol from her pocket and aimed it at his face. He halted, hands up in appeasement.

"Squeaking noises, Ma'am. It sounded like rats." Amberson silently pleaded for Jackson's understanding.

"Look!" Amberson shuddered and swept his arm toward the remains, still exposed in the night air. The ravages of the feeding frenzy were obvious. "It *was* rats, more rats than I'd ever seen before. I beat at them with the shovel to drive them away."

Mrs. Millett lowered the pistol, stepped closer, and peered at Private Massie. The color drained from her face. She made the sign of the cross, mumbled a few words, and then glared at Amberson. Her voice shook with rage, horror, or both. "Why were you burying him, hiding the evidence of this, this violation?" she demanded, pointing the pistol once more. "You didn't think to report the incident?"

"I was only thinking of Private Massie, Ma'am. It would be un-Christian to leave him like this." He looked down and scuffed his toe into the dirt, afraid to meet her eyes. "And a lady shouldn't have to see such a sight."

"Do you really believe me that delicate?" Mrs. Millett stepped toward him and shook a finger in his face. "After running this hospital for two years I can assure you I have an iron constitution." She paced, waving the pistol in the air as she spoke. "Desecrating a grave is a serious offense."

"I know where the rats went!" Amberson said. He needed to remain free to serve his general. The mischief was expendable. "I saw them run that way." He pointed to the west, toward the clearing. "Please. You must believe me."

"No, Sergeant, I do not believe you. You've become quite a problem over the past weeks. Now I discover..." She gestured toward the disturbed earth and sighed. "I must be able to depend on my orderlies. I believe it's time for you to return to your unit."

Amberson's pulse pounded in his ears. He'd hoped to serve out the war at the hospital. He'd be unable to protect Jackson from the front.

"Mrs. Millett, please. If the rats are where I think they are, we can kill many of them at once. They will likely be too sated to move quickly. Let me show you." He shouldered the shovel and backed toward the woods, never taking his eyes off her.

Mrs. Millett frowned and rubbed her temples. "Very well. But only because you showed such early promise. If what you say is true and we can finally rid the hospital of these pests, perhaps you may stay on." She dropped the pistol to her side and followed his lead.

Amberson's heart sang with hope. He wouldn't have to leave after all! He pushed aside low-hanging branches and led the way into the clearing. The empty clearing. Empty but for the glint of a pair of small blue eyes in the bushes to the left.

"This is where they went, I swear!" He avoided looking toward Jackson.

Mrs. Millett stepped into the center of the clearing and turned a slow circle. "The grass is trampled," she said. "Something was here. But there is no evidence of rats." She shook her head. "I'm sorry Sergeant Amberson, but it seems my first instinct was correct. The incident at the grave must be fully investigated. Please return with me." She raised the pistol once more, using it to gesture toward the hospital.

Suddenly, Jackson sprinted out of the bushes directly toward Mrs. Millett. She screamed and pointed the gun at the rat.

"Stop!" shouted Amberson. In two long steps, he tackled Mrs. Millett, pushing her to the ground and wresting the pistol away. Jackson stood mere inches from the woman's face, back arched and hissing.

"Lie still! He won't hurt you," Amberson promised.

She opened her mouth to scream, but before Amberson could slap his hand over her mouth to silence her, the rat squirmed between her lips and clamped onto her tongue. Her scream was reduced to a gurgle. As if that were the signal, the rest of the mischief boiled out of the surrounding woods, dozens upon dozens of rats clambering over both people.

"No!" shouted Amberson, struggling to his feet. The rats fell off as he rose, none of them attempting to bite or cling to him. Mrs. Millett was not so fortunate, as the grey bodies quickly became streaked with red. The poor woman! Her muffled moans of pain were nearly drowned out by the wet sounds and squeaks of the feeding mischief.

Amberson aimed the pistol at a cluster of rats running toward her and pulled the trigger, only to have it misfire. Remembering the shovel, he retrieved it and swatted away as many furry bodies as he could reach. The rat army finally stopped when Jackson let out a high-pitched series of squeaks, raised his left front leg, and led them back into the woods.

Amberson stood panting, leaning on the shovel and looking down at the motionless woman. He knelt and felt a weak pulse in her neck. Relieved, he drew back his hand and wiped her blood on his trousers. Mercifully, she had lost consciousness. In addition to her tongue, the rats had taken the matron's eyes, all the fingers on her right hand, and the thumb and forefinger of her left hand. But Jackson had remained honorable and did not allow his followers to kill her.

Amberson picked up the matron and carried her back to the hospital, with a quick stop to rebury Private Massie. He then "found" her on the lower back porch and called for help. Of course, he knew nothing about what had happened to the unfortunate woman.

After three days in the hospital, Mrs. Millett's sister arrived from Georgia and whisked her away to recover from her injuries, so she was never able to tell of the night's events.

Despite the removal of Mrs. Millett, Amberson was indeed redeployed. One week after the matron was injured, the doctors declared Sergeant Amberson well enough to return to the field. The reluctant soldier was rounded up, along with a half-dozen other men, to join General Johnson's Stonewall Division in Orange County.

On the morning of his redeployment, Sergeant Amberson made certain he was the last soldier to board the northbound transport train, flicking his eyes left and right as he mounted the step. A whiskery face with striking blue eyes poked out of his rucksack, chittered loudly, then ducked back inside the warm nest. As the doors of the railcar slid slowly closed, several small shadows darted aboard.

CHEESE COURSE - WEE FOLK

Recommended Wine: Dry Rosé

THE SUCCESSION

Cleo knelt in front of the weed, wrapped her hand around it, and yanked. Her fingers slid up the plant, stripping all the prickly leaves but leaving the stalk firmly in the ground.

"Dammit," she said and sucked on her sore index finger.

"I'm gonna win, you bitch." She used both hands on the stalk and leaned away from the weed until the taproot gave up its grip, bringing up a large clump of clay and toppling her onto her butt. Weeds clung to soil like limpets to rocks. Or certain people to prizes. She wiped a hand across her sweaty forehead, leaving a smear of soil and a little blood.

Her satisfaction was short-lived, however, when she looked at her garden. Ten tomato plants were lined up in two rows of five, spaced six feet apart and enclosed by tall, square cages. All heirlooms, or at least potential heirlooms. Right now, they had shriveled leaves, and a few of the fruits had blossom-end rot. Some of the plants had no fruits at all, not even green.

A buzzing sound to her left, like a hummingbird, startled her. She turned to see a tiny, pale woman hovering at eye level. The woman was about six inches tall and wore a light-green toga. She had long, fine white hair, and a youthful face, with dazzling emerald eyes. Her smile displayed a mouthful of pointy little teeth.

"Orrla," said Cleo, relieved. She glanced toward the house. They were alone. "Boy am I glad to see you." She gestured at her garden. "Look at them." Tears of frustration welled.

Orrla flew to the nearest tomato plant, a Brandywine, folded her gossamer wings, and sat on its upper branches with her legs dangling. She glanced down the row of plants and shook her head. A frown wrinkled her forehead when she met Cleo's eyes.

"I've weeded, I've watered, I've fertilized. I've done everything humanly possible. Help," said Cleo.

"It's okay, Klee O," said Orrla. "I will help them." Her voice was musical; she almost sang her words. She flew around each plant, touching the fruit and stroking the leaves. Then she landed and moved between them, sprinkling a sparkly red substance around the roots that shimmered on top of the soil for a few seconds before being absorbed.

Orrla flew straight up and hovered in front of Cleo. She curtsied in midair. "All done," she said with a smile.

"Thank you so much," said Cleo. "Again. I don't know what I'd do without you." She swept her hand toward the plants. "They look better already."

Orrla's eyes caught Cleo's still-bleeding index finger, and she slid her small tongue around her lips. "You're hurt," she said. "Let me help." She flew closer.

Cleo clenched her hand into a fist and covered it with the other hand. "No really, you've done so much already. I...I'll be fine."

"Okay, if you're sure," said the pixie, hovering for an extra few seconds before she sighed and flew into the woods.

Cleo shuffled back to the house, thinking that Orrla always showed up just when Cleo was desperate. She appreciated the help at the time. The second thoughts came later.

Her arthritic knees ached, aggravated by the extra 30 pounds she was carrying. But, at sixty-three years old, she wasn't about to give up her comfort foods. She loved her nightly bowl of ice cream and her full-sugar sodas. And she kept a supply of chocolates in the kitchen drawer.

She'd always been chubby and mostly ordinary-looking: medium brown hair, medium brown eyes, of medium height. Two characteristics were not medium—her shapely legs (still shapely, even with the extra weight) and (unfortunately offsetting the legs) an oversized bulbous nose. It was as though she'd been assembled from spare parts.

After her mother died, Cleo legally shortened her name from the optimistic "Cleopatra" and joined a dating service. She was looking for a kind, intelligent man—looks unimportant. Unfortunately, it seemed no men considered looks unimportant. She dug into her work, knowing she would have to take care of herself.

She'd retired three years earlier from a long career as a bookkeeper with the transportation department of the Hadley County Schools. She had savings enough to supplement her government pension and maintain a comfortable lifestyle. Gardening was a means to save money on groceries and she was good at it. When she decided on a whim to enter some of her produce in a contest (and won), she discovered a fierce competitive streak.

She planned to enter her current crop of heirloom tomatoes at the Hadley County Agricultural Fair. Not only was there a small cash prize, but the win came with a title—Tomato Queen (or King). This was her third year, and she'd come close last year with an honorable mention. She was determined to seize both title and bragging rights this year.

She'd just finished feeding Eddie, her medium-size brown mutt, when she heard a knock followed by the creak of the front door swinging open.

"Yoo hoo, it's just me."

"Hi, Barb. In the kitchen," she called, reminding herself to lock the door.

Her neighbor bustled in carrying a large glass platter. A layer cake with white icing perched in the center of it.

"I'm returning your platter, but I brought a cake with it to say thanks. It's your favorite, spice cake," said Barb. She sat the heavy platter on the table and herself in a chair, wincing and shifting to the right before leaning against the backrest. "So, been out in the garden?" She gestured at her own perfectly made-up forehead and pointed at Cleo.

Cleo grabbed a paper towel, wet it, and scrubbed the garden soil off her forehead. "Thanks," she said with a smile. "Those tomatoes don't grow themselves. At least not the prize-winning ones."

"Don't I know it," said Barb. "I'm out there every day. But it's *so* worth it to win the crown at the fair." She was the reigning Tomato Queen and had won the last two years in a row.

"Well, I wouldn't know about that," said Cleo. Out there every day my ass. The woman isn't even sweaty, perfect manicure as usual. She *had* to have paid help.

"I'm sure you'll win, eventually. Your tomatoes are always so beautiful," said Barb, with a saccharine smile. "But I'll give you a run for your money." Eddie snuffled at her lap and she scooted to the right, resting both hands on the table. She had cats. Lots of them.

"You enjoy the cake, hon, I've got to scamper," Barb said, pushing herself up from the chair. "Toodles!" The door slammed behind her.

Cleo waited a minute. Then she locked the door and turned to see the dog watching her with his ears perked up. Well, one ear perked up. The other stuck straight out to the side.

"She only wins because she's younger than me," said Cleo. "Isn't that right, Eddie?"

Eddie thumped his tail in agreement.

"That's okay, boy. This year we have a secret weapon."

Thump, thump.

Cleo met Barb four years before she retired, when her husband, Andrew, replaced Cleo's longtime boss, Frank. At Frank's going-away luncheon, Barb kept her adoring gaze on her husband, like a wannabe Nancy Reagan. She'd never held a job and her life revolved around him. She picked at her food, claiming she wasn't hungry. Cleo cleaned her plate and finished with two pieces of chocolate cake.

Despite their differences, Cleo and Barb developed a casual friendship. Cleo appreciated Barb's wicked sense of humor, and they met for lunch every month or so. They made quite the odd couple, as Barb was petite, pretty, and stylish. She also was insecure, always asking about the latest college interns and how much time her husband spent with them. Cleo secretly thought part of the reason Barb liked her was that she posed no threat.

When Andrew died of a heart attack the year Cleo retired, Barb was shattered and leaned heavily on her. They'd had no children and Barb had no family living in the area. Cleo tried to be supportive, but she found such neediness foreign and a bit oppressive. After all, she'd been alone since her mother died. Fortunately, after a few months Barb regained her bearings and Cleo was relieved to see less of her. Cleo's life returned to its normal, quiet routine. Until two years ago.

The old Henson place had been on the market for some time with no takers. Barb, who'd always lived in town, decided she wanted to try the country life and bought the house. Two doors down from Cleo. She'd respected boundaries, for the most part, and Cleo had to admit it was nice to talk to someone other than Eddie.

Despite her lack of gardening experience, Barb had won the Tomato Queen title right out of the gate. Twice. Cleo tried to jolly her out of the secret to her success.

"A lady never tells," Barb said, wagging her finger.

Cleo pulled off her sweaty gardening clothes. She hissed with pain when she removed her bra, avoiding the three small Band-Aids that surrounded her left nipple. In the shower, she peeled them off and carefully cleaned each dime-size wound. After she had dried herself, she looked longingly at the box of Band-Aids but left the wounds uncovered.

Naked, she walked to her bedroom, opened the window, and slid between the sheets. Her heart raced with dread. She was tired from the day, though, and sleep overtook her within minutes.

A tug on the side of her left breast pulled her out of a dream. She heard the buzzing of small wings and opened her eyes. The sheet was pulled down to her waist and she watched while Orrla applied her pointy teeth, tore off a small chunk of skin and chewed vigorously. Cleo could neither move nor feel pain because of the paralyzing and anesthetic effect of the pixie's saliva. She closed her eyes and waited for it to be over, oddly disconnected from her own body.

She'd first met Orrla last fall, while walking with Eddie. She had just passed the old oak tree when he trotted out of the woods and dropped a pale creature at her feet. She thought it might be an albino squirrel. She bent for a closer look, took off her glasses, rubbed them with her t-shirt, and looked again. It was slippery from dog slobber, but there were no obvious injuries. It was female, and exquisitely beautiful.

The creature introduced herself as Orrla and told Cleo that Eddie had saved her from a hungry fox. She recuperated in Cleo's house for two days, consumed an amazing amount of fresh vegetables and fruits for one so small, and educated Cleo about her kind. Pixies form tribes, she said, and each tribe cares for a specific area of land, ensuring that the vegetation is healthy and productive. Orrla was the leader of her tribe. When the pixie asked how she could repay Cleo for her kindness, all Cleo could think of was next year's Fair. And "Queen" Barb.

A small tongue lapping the new wound returned her to the present. The lapping stopped and Cleo opened her eyes, hoping the pixie was gone. Orrla moved to one of the existing wounds and scraped the scab off, causing it to seep. Cleo closed her eyes again and felt Orrla lapping the old sore. She revisited each existing wound and continued to feed. The feeding stopped and Cleo heard the buzzing of wings and felt a faint breeze on her face.

"Klee O," sang Orrla.

Cleo opened her eyes. Orrla hovered in front of her. Her pale skin had taken on a rosy tone. She was terrifyingly beautiful.

"You will win the crown," said Orrla. She flashed a blood-tinged smile and flew out the window.

After a few moments, Cleo wiggled her fingers and toes, testing her ability to move again. She felt faintly nauseated, as she always did after Orrla fed. Once she'd cleaned and bandaged the wounds, though, visions of lush green plants weighed down with perfect fruit flooded her thoughts and brought a smile. Winning the title would make her sacrifice worthwhile.

The next day the garden was transformed. The tomato plants were thriving. There were more immature fruits on each plant than yesterday, and the ripe ones were larger and more luscious. Cleo clapped her hands, squealed when she accidentally hit her sore left breast, and then laughed. Between the antiseptic ointment and the sight of her perfect tomato plants, the pain was nearly forgotten.

When Cleo had first asked for Orrla's help, the pixie had explained that she could make Cleo's garden produce healthy, ordinary tomatoes. But she could do more, if Cleo wished. Exceptional tomatoes were possible, but the process depleted her energy and required special food.

Cleo had been horrified at the cost and could never imagine agreeing to that price. But in the spring, after she planted her seedlings, disaster struck in the form of a fungus. She started over, only to have beetles attack. At the height of her frustration, Orrla appeared and offered to help. Cleo gave in. But only under the condition that her "payments" to Orrla be in an area hidden by clothing.

Cleo put the finishing touches on her artistic display and stood back to admire her handiwork. The lush ripeness of the fruits and the variety of their colors—pink, red, yellow, purple—were gorgeous. She waited until just before the judging to slice one of each variety and plate them in front of the basket of whole fruits. She leaned over the glistening slices and breathed in their sweet, tangy aroma. She knew the taste was heavenly. It had taken two more visits from Orrla, but these tomatoes were perfect.

"Yoo hoo!" Barb was heading straight for her, favoring her left leg. She wore a hunter green, color-coordinated pantsuit. The dark color made her look more pale than usual.

Cleo forced a smile. "Barb! Did you pull a muscle?" Maybe she *did* actually do some work in the garden. Nails are still perfect though.

"Oh no, just a little stiffness. I'll be fine." Barb stopped in front of Cleo's table and leaned against it.

"Today's the big day. Are you ready?" said Cleo.

"Of course! I just had to see how yours turned out." Barb looked at the fruit, running her fingers lightly across their skin and hmm hmming. "Lovely, Cleo. You've outdone yourself." She put out her hand. "Good luck. I think it'll be close this year."

"Good luck to you as well. As if you need it," Cleo said with a fleeting smile. She rounded the table and looped her arm through her neighbor's. "It's only fair I get to see yours too."

As they approached Barb's table, it was obvious who the real competitors were. All the other displays of tomatoes were average at best. The two standouts were Cleo and Barb.

"Beautiful, Barb. We can both be proud of our hard work." Cleo knew *she'd* worked hard.

Barb sank into a chair behind her table, closed her eyes, and pinched the bridge of her nose. She looked up with a weak smile. "Well, I for one will be glad when it's over. This season has really taken it out of me." She straightened in her chair and patted her perfectly styled (and dyed) hair. "This may well be my last year competing. I don't know how *you* keep going, Cleo."

"Just tough stock, I suppose." Bitch.

Peggy Thrasher, the head judge, strode toward Cleo. "Please bring your display to the front table," she said. She pivoted and walked away without looking back.

Cleo balanced her basket and plate and trailed in Mrs. Thrasher's wake. Barb was already at the front table with her wares displayed.

"We're the finalists! Isn't it exciting?" Barb beamed.

"Yes, it is," said Cleo, twisting her sweaty hands together. She felt light-headed.

They stood side by side behind their displays as Mrs. Thrasher conferred with the other two judges. Barb grabbed Cleo's hand. Cleo took deep breaths and watched the judges. Mrs. Thrasher frowned and shook her head.

All three came back for another look and then stepped away again. The two other judges seemed to be making an argument to the head judge, who finally sighed and nodded.

Mrs. Thrasher stood in front of the table, hands clasped at her ample waist. One judge stood next to her with ribbon and sash in hand. The other judge jogged up with a matching ribbon and sash.

Cleo's stomach sank.

"This has never happened before," began Mrs. Thrasher, "but we can't decide. You both have such perfect tomatoes." She waved the other two judges forward.

Cleo watched in disbelief as a blue ribbon was placed on each display. She lifted her numb arms to allow the judge to put a sash around her, wincing when the woman bumped her left side. The other judge put a sash around Barb. Both sashes had a picture of a golden crown, followed by the year.

She pasted on a smile while silently screaming, No! I don't want to share.

Cleo pulled the newspaper from the box and glared at the front page as she trudged back to the house. There with their arms around each other, smiles frozen in place, were Cleo and Barb, the co-Tomato Queens of the County Fair.

She was almost to her front door, still fuming, when she did an about-face and strode down the street. She was going to have a little chat with Barb and find out exactly how she got her results.

Cleo rapped her knuckles against her neighbor's front door, not noticing it was unlatched until it swung inward. "Barb?"

A cat purred and wrapped itself around her legs as she hesitated in the silent hallway. Barb always had the TV or radio or some noise going. Kept her company she said. A clock ticked.

Another cat perched in the doorway to the kitchen, licking its paws. A trail of dark paw prints led down the hall toward the bedroom. Cleo frowned and peeked into the kitchen. Empty. The bedroom door was slightly ajar. A third cat sprinted out of her way with a yowl as she pushed the door open.

A metallic smell hit her nostrils, pushed by the breeze lifting the curtains from the open window. Barb lay naked and face-down on top of the covers, motionless. Something on the lower half of her body was moving. Cleo flipped the light switch and froze. A swarm of pixies pushed at each other like nursing puppies, heads down and buried in Barb's left buttock. Blood covered the tiny bodies, turning them from white to red. Another pair of pixies was working on her right calf. The toes on her left foot were gone. The darkened sheets told of more injuries not visible.

Cleo remembered Barb's limp. And her pallor.

"Orrla?" Her voice shook as shivers racked her body. She swallowed repeatedly, trying not to throw up.

A crimson figure flew up from the scrum. Red droplets from her wings sprayed Cleo's face.

"Queen Klee O," sang the pixie queen. Orrla seemed delighted to welcome her to the sisterhood, displaying her bloodstained teeth in a wide grin.

Cleo fled.

She locked her front and back doors, and closed all the windows. Her left breast throbbed. She sat trembling at the kitchen table, Eddie watching her with his ears perked up.

Think, Cleo, think!

If they drove far enough, they would be out of the pixies' territory. But this was her home; she couldn't just leave and not come back.

Buzzing sounded from the hallway. Orrla flew in, followed by four of her tribe. Their bodies had turned from red to black. The chimney!

"Queen Klee O," sang Orrla. "We mean you no harm."

"What about Barb?" Cleo picked up Eddie and backed into a corner.

"She broke the agreement. She was punished." Orrla's green eyes glimmered in her black face. "You won!" The pixie looked puzzled.

Horror, happiness, and fear waltzed around her mind. What had Barb done wrong? Cleo had meticulously upheld *her* end of the agreement (she believed). She swallowed hard.

"Thank you," Cleo said, just wanting them to leave. "I'm grateful."

Orrla clapped her tiny hands. "Good. See you next year." The dark cloud of pixies followed their queen out of the room.

Cleo's legs failed and she slid down the wall, holding Eddie in her lap. She would enjoy her reign, but the price had been too high. She would politely decline to continue next year.

If Queen Orrla would allow it.

SHINY OBJECTS

Father whirled and peered into the darkness beyond his torch. I flattened against the side of the tunnel, willing myself to blend into the earthen walls. He paused and tilted his head, grunted, and moved on. My soft-soled boots made no sound as I crept behind, staying just beyond the circle of light. He stopped and slid the torch into a slot in the wall, then drove his pick into the roof of the tunnel.

The "thunk" confirmed my worst fear—wood. Four more whacks and he was in. Unsheathing a wickedly curved knife from his belt, he reached into the hole, grabbed something, and sawed. After some time and much effort, I heard a snap, and he pulled a large object from the hole—a partially decomposed human hand with a ruby ring on one finger and an emerald ring on another. From fingertips to wrist stub, the hand was a third as tall as Father, and he had always been on the tall side for a gnome. A wide smile split his beard as he wiggled the rings off the hand and stashed them in his pockets. He dropped the now-unadorned hand on the floor of the tunnel and hoisted himself into the hole above.

The scene in front of me was all too familiar. Father's obsession with gold and gems was getting stronger. The grave robbing started fifty years ago, when it was easier to find caskets not enclosed in steel or concrete vaults and more common for humans to be buried wearing valuable jewelry. This cache was a jackpot.

After Father disappeared into the hole, I retraced my steps through the tunnels back to the village. I could do nothing while he was in the throes of his obsession. After many twists and turns, I exited into the village square. My twin brother, Jurgen, paced in front of the opening.

"Was he at it again?" His eyes were creased with worry.

I nodded. "He was still foraging when I left."

Jurgen touched my nose, sore from the last time I got between Father and his prize. The swelling made us less than identical.

"Horst, you must be careful. If he gets caught, we'll need to care for Mother."

"That won't be necessary because we're going to save him."

I wrapped my arm around his shoulders, and we walked to our cottage. Mother would have dinner ready, even though Father wouldn't be home until after dark. All the better to hide his activities from the rest of the village.

Mother had just cleared the dishes when Father swaggered through the front door, pockets sagging and jingling. A whiff of putrefaction clung to his clothing.

"Renata, my love," he boomed, slapping her on the behind.

She squealed and darted to the other side of the table. He leered and gave chase, but she was too quick and managed to keep the table between them.

"Fritz, not in front of the boys," she said, blushing, but smiling all the same.

Jurgen and I rolled our eyes. We were 172 years old, far from boys. But to our 300-year-old mother, we would always be her boys. And we were well aware of Father's appetites. The walls of the cottage were not thick enough to muffle his almost nightly cries of delight. Or hers. It's a wonder we were the only offspring.

Father gave up the chase and dug into his pockets.

"Wait!" I hurried to close the shutters.

He pulled out two familiar rings, a necklace of emeralds, and a pair of ruby earrings, and placed them on the table.

"Jewels for my jewel," he said, sweeping his arm over the display.

"They're lovely, Fritz," Mother said. She frowned and didn't move toward the jewelry. "But I thought you said you were done with..."

"I know, I know," Father said, waving his hand. "But I happened to sniff these out, purely by accident. Couldn't very well leave them there. The prior owner wasn't using them anymore." His satisfied grin made him look decades younger than his 305 years.

He was lying, of course. He'd been tunneling toward this latest stash for two weeks. I'd seen the circled obituary of the wealthy woman. I followed him the night he went above ground to make certain of the grave's location.

While Father was in the washroom, we gathered around the table and stared at the jewels.

"They are beautiful," Mother said, reaching for one of the rings.

I pushed her hand away. "No! You know you can't wear them. You know the penalty."

"But I didn't take them," she wailed. "Oh, why does he tempt me so?"

Jurgen put his arm around her. "We can appreciate their beauty without owning them. They must be returned."

"But no one will ever know they're missing!" she said, weeping.

She was wrong.

Our family was one of the oldest in the village, going back four generations. My great- grandfather Lothar had stowed away with his wife on a ship from Germany and settled in rural Virginia. He was escaping persecution for whom he had married—great-grandmother Gerta was not a pure-blooded gnome. A troll had raped her mother, and

Gerta was the result. Though she looked like a gnome, her heritage was common knowledge and the rest of the villagers shunned her.

Trolls are long-time enemies of gnomes. They are vile, selfish, greedy, and smelly. One of their more disturbing traits is an obsession with gold and gems. A troll on the trail of treasure has been known to go without food for weeks. Gerta had the obsession, but Lothar kept it at bay by ensuring her a steady supply of jewelry. Despite being only one-eighth troll, however, our father's obsession was strong and had only increased through the years.

Jurgen and I covered for him by returning what he stole; if we could discover where it came from. Once he acquired a piece, he mostly lost interest. For him, the thrill was in the hunt. He stashed his treasures in a locked storage room where he would occasionally fondle the jewels and admire the way they caught the light. Jurgen made copies of the pieces and I replaced the originals so Father wouldn't notice.

Jurgen had done an exceptionally fast job recreating the latest booty. Two days after the theft, I set off to return the pilfered items. Father was ensconced in the pub for the evening, regaling his friends with tall tales.

"Be careful," Jurgen said. He always fretted when I went on these trips, though not enough to join me.

I followed the twisting route back to the scene of the crime, once taking a wrong turn and being forced to backtrack. Nerves must have been affecting my usually excellent memory. When I arrived at the dark hole in the roof of the tunnel, I noticed that the hand Father had discarded was partially covered by fresh soil. Strange. I placed my torch in the holder and picked up the hand, tossing it up and over the edge of the opening, then pulled myself up and through the hole. Moonlight glowed all around me. There was no trace of the casket or its contents. I stood at the bottom of an open, empty grave.

"Detective Esteves," said the medical examiner, "are you all right in there?"

Esteves leaned under the faucet, filled his mouth with water, and spat into the sink. The taste of vomit was still present, but not as bad. He fished a stick of gum from his pocket, thankful for the habit that had replaced cigarettes.

"Coming," he said and returned to the autopsy.

A woman lay in several pieces on the table. That had gotten to him. This was his first exhumation—she'd been in the ground for three weeks. Her head had been severed, her right hand was missing, and both ears had been torn from her head.

"Okay now, princess?" Malone, the lead detective, smirked. Esteves hadn't helped himself lose the rookie stench.

"Good," he mumbled. "Let's finish."

"All injuries are postmortem," Doc Simmons said. "The removal of the head appears to have been done in one motion with no stopping or sawing. Could be a large, very sharp blade or a wire of some sort." He lifted the corpse's right arm. "On the other hand..." He grinned at his own joke. "The hand was sawed off, more brute force than skill. Like the ears."

"Any chance an animal could have done this?" asked Esteves.

Malone rolled his eyes.

"Not unless it had thumbs," Doc Simmons said.

"But the hole in the casket was too small for a person," Esteves said, trying to salvage his argument. "We've got to consider all possibilities."

"Tell you what, sunshine," Malone said. "You just earned yourself the lead on the grave robbing and corpse mutilation. I'll keep after the husband. His alibi for when the wife had 'her accident' has evaporated. Never trust a mistress." He snickered and turned his back. "Let me know when you arrest that badger."

Rookie scut work ate up the rest of Detective Esteves' afternoon. But at least the people around him were alive, assuming they'd had their coffee. Malone wouldn't give him any extra manpower unless he came up with a damn good reason. In the meantime, he requisitioned a motion detector with a camera and set it up at the cemetery on the way home.

He arrived home and Slugger met him at the door, wagging her whole body. A tan and white pit bull, they'd rescued each other two years ago. Her looks were the only thing mean about her—this dog was a moosh. He finished dinner and was sitting on the couch watching TV, Slugger's head in his lap as usual, when his cell phone buzzed. Something had tripped the motion detector. Probably an animal. Maybe Malone's badger.

Esteves touched the app on his phone and displayed live video from the detector. An object at the bottom of the grave caught his eye. A miniature person with a beard and a pointy cap. Had someone put a garden gnome in the hole as a sick joke? But then the creature tilted his head to look up. His gaze swept past the camera and the detective's vision blurred. He blinked and refocused on the screen. The gnome kicked something out of his way, then disappeared through a small hole in the grave floor.

Esteves leaned back, heart pounding. What had he just seen? He was stone-cold sober.   Hadn't had a drink in forty-seven days. He figured drinking would make quitting smoking harder than it already was and hadn't really missed it. Until now. He looked at the screen again—nothing but the empty grave. After five minutes, the camera switched to energy-saving mode and went black.

Peaceful evening disturbed, the detective drove to the cemetery and parked as close as possible to the gravesite. Yellow crime scene tape flapped around the opening. Slugger walked quietly by his side. The small motion detector was perched at the foot of the deep hole, angled slightly downward. He clicked on a flashlight and found the gnome's bolt hole, about a foot across and round. From here, he couldn't see how deep it was.

"Shit, I'm gonna have to go down there," he muttered. Esteves dropped Slugger's leash. "Stay," he told the dog. She whined, licked his hand, and slowly lowered her butt to the ground.

Six feet was a long way to jump, not to mention try to climb out. The detective retrieved a coil of rope from the trunk of the car, keeping one eye on the dog. She didn't move but wrinkled her brow at him, looking worried. He tied the rope around the nearest tree, slid the flashlight into his back pocket, and rappelled into the open grave. His light scanned the dark corners and revealed what the gnome had kicked out of the way. Propped against the side of the grave, like it was trying to climb out on its own, was the missing hand.

Esteves gagged, then swallowed, willing himself not to vomit. Pulling an evidence bag out of his pocket, he used it to pick up the hand, then turned the bag inside out to capture it. Just like cleaning up after Slugger.

—◦❖◦—

"What do you mean 'it's gone'?" asked Jurgen.

"Gone. Not there. Nothing but a hole." I shook my head. "I couldn't very well leave the jewels in an empty hole, now could I? That wasn't where he found them."

"They know." Jurgen rubbed his forehead.

"Of course they don't. Humans don't believe we exist, even less so than they used to. They'll blame it on animals."

I shuddered at the thought of the last time humans discovered a gnome village. "The Harrington Massacre" was included in all our history books. The possibility of discovery was the biggest risk Father took, and the main reason the village elders were so strict about grave robbing. All gnomes enjoy shiny objects, but most know where to draw the line.

"But what if they don't blame it on animals? What if they trace the tunnel? Can we fill it in?" Jurgen shot questions at me like bullets.

I smiled. Parallel thoughts between twins are not merely a thing of lore.

We set out the next night. This was the first time Jurgen had accompanied me beyond the entrance to Father's tunnels. He imagined followers behind us at every turn, being unused to the way the tunnels echoed and bent sound. Each of us carried a backpack filled with explosives.

At the the opening in the roof of the tunnel, I held up a hand. "Wait. Listen." Seconds stretched while we rotated our ears left and right.

"Nothing." We whispered the word simultaneously.

I motioned to Jurgen to stay put and hoisted myself through the hole to the floor of the gravesite. A blinding light hit my eyes and a weighted net fell on me.

"Run!" I shouted, struggling to remove my backpack, willing to die in defense of family and village, when a blow to the head plunged me into darkness.

"Looks just like a person, huh girl?" said Esteves.

Slugger growled at the creature in her crate. She pressed her snout against the bars, and the gnome retreated to the other side. He'd lost his pointy cap and blood crusted the edge of his hairline. A thick beard reached halfway down his chest. Standing straight up in the crate, his head was still a couple of inches from the top.

Esteves sat on the edge of a chair, sipping bourbon and leaning toward the makeshift prison cell. Forty-eight days sober had been a good run, but he was quitting smoking, not drinking, and there was a damn good reason to drink looking back at him.

Capturing the little guy had been surprisingly easy; patience went a long way. When Esteves had shown Malone last night's video, he'd accused him of doctoring the recording. The detective couldn't wait to bring in the living, breathing proof tomorrow.

The gnome grimaced and rubbed his head. A bluish-purple knot stood out on his left temple. "Did you have to hit me so hard?" he asked in a deep voice, unexpected for one so small.

Esteves jumped. "You...you speak English?"

"I speak many languages." The gnome let out a whimper, followed by a couple of yips.

The detective watched in disbelief as his loyal dog stopped growling and commando-crawled toward the gnome, flipped over to expose her belly, and thumped her tail.

"Point proven. So, let's have a chat, shall we?" Esteves reached for his phone to record the interrogation. This case was going in a direction he never expected.

"Detective Paul Esteves interviewing..." He nodded toward the prisoner. "State your name."

"Horst. Horst Madder." The gnome scratched his beard and looked directly at the man for the first time. He had the most incredible sea-green eyes. Hypnotic.

"Nice to meet you, Paul." Horst stuck his hand through the bars of the crate. Esteves shook the small hand.

"We haven't much time," said Horst, and looked away.

Released from the gnome's gaze, the detective stared at the melting ice cubes in his drink. He was definitely buzzed, but those eyes! They were deep enough to swim in. He gave himself a mental shake.

"Oh, we've got all night."

"You don't understand. My family will come for me and they will be angry. You really don't want to meet my father when he's angry."

Esteves drained the last of the bourbon and focused on a spot just over the gnome's shoulder, careful not to meet his eyes. "I think I can handle a few more 'little people'."

Horst winced and shook his head. "You have no idea. But if you let me go now, I'll forget this ever happened. I'll return the stolen jewels and promise there won't be any more grave robbing in your district."

If Esteves returned the jewels, he'd be a hero. Of course, he'd have to explain how he found them and come up with a theory about who had stolen them. And he couldn't tell anyone, much less Malone, that there would be no more grave robbing. If that was even true. The gnome would say anything to get out of here. No, the original plan was still the best.

"So, you admit you stole the jewels. I think I'll pass on your deal. I can get the goods back without selling my soul, *and* I'll have a perp in custody. Wait here." Like he had a choice. The detective chuckled and went to the kitchen for a refill.

On the way, he stopped in the bathroom to take a long piss, making room for the fresh drink. Ice cubes rattled from the dispenser, and he topped them with lovely, caramel-colored liquid. A thumping noise from the living room made him quicken his steps to the hallway.

The thumping noise was Slugger's tail. She lay sprawled on her side with a silly grin on her face. The door to the crate stood open and Horst was scratching her ears. Two other gnomes wearing backpacks stood behind her, one who looked just like Horst, and an older one. A trail of small, muddy boot prints led into the living room from the back door.

"My son tells me you have spoken to others about us," the old gnome said. "And that you plan to take him to jail tomorrow."

He pierced Esteves with his eyes, dark blue, like an angry ocean before a storm. The man's surroundings blurred so that all he saw were twin blue orbs.

"Yeah, that's right," said the detective, pretending swagger he didn't feel. A single gnome in a crate was one thing, but three unrestrained? He tried to tear his eyes away but couldn't. He swallowed hard.

The old gnome stepped close to Slugger and rubbed her belly with a small hand, setting off another round of ecstatic tail thumping.

"This is a nice dog. There's never been a dog who killed a gnome or wiped out his family and village." The creature flared its nostrils. "Can't say that about humans."

Esteves stood frozen. He couldn't look away from those eyes or move a muscle. What was happening? He felt like a statue.

"First, you need to write a note."

The muscles in his head and neck released. "Yes, yes, whatever you want," he said, nodding like a fucking bob-blehead. The gnome released the rest of his body, and he scrabbled in the drawer for a pen, snatching up the phone-side notepad. He'd gone from statue to puppet.

"Write exactly what I say."

Esteves' mind raced as his traitorous hands wrote the confession. How would he explain this when he got out of this mess? *If* he got out of this mess?

The old gnome reached into his backpack and removed a velvet drawstring bag, the kind jewelers use. It chinked when he lifted it, the bottom pulled down by the weight of its contents. He took the completed note, put it on the coffee table, and tossed the bag on top.

"Now, follow the boys." He nodded at Horst and the other gnome. "Take your cell phone," he added, wagging his finger.

Horst gave the detective a pitying look. "I tried to warn you. You should have taken my offer."

The group halted in the garage, where the old gnome commanded Esteves to toss the cell phone on the floor in front of Jurgen. Esteves watched his last hope shatter with one swing of a sledgehammer.

The younger gnomes led the man into the backyard, where a large hole had appeared. Horst's brother disap-peared into it.

"After you," Horst said, bowing deeply.

Esteves' body climbed in while his mind screamed in protest. Even though he wasn't locked in the gaze of a gnome, they still held him in thrall. He crouched at the bottom of the hole, then squeezed into a tunnel where the lead gnome held a torch. The others climbed in behind and he saw the glow from their torches as his body crawled down the dank, musty tunnel. His mind returned to Slugger—at least they hadn't harmed her.

Jurgen led the way, with me and Father bringing up the rear. Literally, as we had to look at the man's ass while he crawled through tunnels we easily walked through.

I almost felt sorry for Esteves. He'd begun to sob while he crawled, occasionally begging to be taken back to his house. After getting no response, he begged to be let back above ground and he would clear all this up. When we reached our destination, the detective slumped against the wall of the tunnel, tears streaming and chest heaving.

"You're almost getting your wish, Detective," Father said. "You won't be quite so deep underground."

Jurgen and I swung our picks at the roof of the tunnel, opening a larger hole than usual. We struck wood at the same time and worked until we cleared a large entry to the hollow space above.

"I hope this goes quickly, Detective. I bear you no ill will. My duty is to protect my family." I leaned on my pick and gestured toward the opening. "Climb in."

The man's eyes were wild and panicked. He shook his head from side to side even as his arms rose to hoist himself into the casket. A desiccated femur fell to the floor of the tunnel. Jurgen tossed it back in before we started to fill in the opening.

After three turns through the maze of tunnels leading back to the village, I could no longer hear his screams.

DESSERT - THE AFTER TIMES

Recommended Wine: Reisling

WHEELS AGAINST WINGS

Charlie rolled toward the racetrack, absorbing bumps from the uneven ground with his relaxed upper body. The sturdy cross-country wheels worked as designed and he remained upright. An extra blast of steam trailed behind him like a pennant as he powered toward the top of the steep hill. Traces of morning mist hovered in the crisp air.

Crowds lined either side of the track. A cacophony of cheers and clanging metal arose to greet him.

"Look! It's him. My money's on Old Charlie."

He waved to the crowd, shot a quick glance at one of two large tents, then rolled toward the other. A guard stood in front of the tightly closed flaps of his competitor's tent with arms crossed, the left arm under the right mechanical one. Brass and gears made up the length of the arm, which ended in a wicked-looking scimitar. The hybrid guard followed Charlie's movement with his glowing red left eye.

The orb squeaked with each movement. *Hmm, she's not maintaining her staff*, he thought.

His assistant, Winston, waited in the tent.

"Ready to go, boss?" he asked, a wrench in his hand.

"Yep."

Charlie wheeled onto the lift and Winston cranked the handle.

"What are the oddsmakers saying?" Charlie asked. His weight shifted onto the lift when his wheels left the ground.

"Close, but you're still ahead." Winston removed the front set of cross-country wheels. There were some jobs where human limbs were still superior.

"Shouldn't even be close," grumbled Charlie. "Phil would be nowhere without me. The insolence!"

"Confidence, not insolence." Winston pulled off the other pair of wheels and reached for the front set of shiny rail wheels. "She's a chip off the old block."

Was that admiration in his voice? "Whose side are you on?" snapped Charlie. "She needs to be taught her place."

Charlie's youngest daughter and last surviving child, Philomena, had challenged him to today's race. The winner would earn the respect, and the position of Chief, of the Ros. The Ros were one of the larger tribes in what used to be New Mexico in what used to be the United States. *United.* Nothing was united anymore. Not since the people had divided into factions and torn each other apart in defense of their unyielding beliefs. A few cherished books remained that told of a time when people engaged in civilized debates rather than bloody battles.

Winston tightened the last of the bolts on the rear set of wheels. "It's too bad it's come to this. She was an excellent lieutenant." He sighed, and wiped grease off his forehead with the back of his hand. "I miss her."

A pang of regret broke through Charlie's wall of anger. Phil had been the light of his life, blessed with her mother's beauty and her father's strength. And most importantly, unlike her brother and sister, she had survived the enhancement surgeries.

Winston dropped lumps of coal into the storage area above the firebox attached to Charlie's chair, ensuring plenty of fuel for the race ahead. One of the few benefits of the blasted landscape had been the creation of fossil fuels in mere decades instead of eons. The rapid and devastating loss of plant and animal (including human) life during the wars created extremely dense and long-burning coal.

Next, Winston topped off the water reservoir that fed the boiler. Finally, he rolled the lift to the twin rails that began at the corner of the tent. He cranked the lift down until Charlie's wheels settled on them with a soft clink.

Charlie moved back and forth, testing the smooth mechanism of his racing wheels. Engine pistons churned and warm steam floated up the stack running along his spine and out through his top hat. "Good," he grunted.

He was sure that Phil would be just as meticulous with her pre-race checks, despite the condition of her guard. She would put her resources where they counted—ensuring victory for herself and vengeance for her mother.

Charlie's lips tightened at the memory of his wife, splayed in abandon in Edgar's bed, his best friend's arm draped across her perfect breasts. Neither had expected his early return from battle. For a moment he'd frozen in the doorway, disbelief stealing his breath away as he stared at the sleeping pair. He remembered little after that until coming out of the nightmare covered in blood not his own. Lorene and Edgar would never betray him again.

He went before the Council of Elders and explained what he'd found. They had nodded and agreed that the punishment suited the crime. He suffered no consequences for his actions. At least none from the tribe. But the death of her mother launched Philomena on a quest to become strong enough to challenge him and take away his power, the only thing of consequence left in his life.

A flute trilled from outside the tent, summoning the racers. Charlie checked the gold buttons on his vest and secured his top hat. Winston lifted the tent flap and Charlie rolled toward the starting line, keeping his gaze fixed on the horizon. A whoosh of wings came from his right and a breeze ruffled his beard. He turned his head to meet his daughter's eyes, but she wasn't looking at him, instead smiling and waving at the gathered crowd. Large mechanical wings sprouted from her shoulders, covered with white feathers for the occasion. She wore a pure white tunic with silver trim. Mechanical silver talons at the ends of her muscular legs clutched a large wooden beam. She was magnificent!

Finally, she looked at him, her golden eyes a startling contrast to her jet-black hair. Hair like her mother's. But those golden eyes were as cold as a raptor's. A chill ran down his spine.

She nodded. "Charlie."

He returned the nod, "Philomena." She hadn't called him father since Lorene's death.

Stevenson, the head Elder, stood in front of the pair. "Are the racers ready?" he asked, addressing the seconds.

Winston spoke first. "Yes, sir. Mechanically sound and ready to go."

Hawkins, Phil's hybrid second, waved his mechanical arm toward his mistress. "Mechanically sound *and* beautiful. Is she not?" he said, playing to the crowd, which roared its agreement.

Steam shot from Charlie's hat. He shook his head. All that show would be for naught after the race. A pretty appearance may temporarily charm the people, but a strong victory would win their loyalty.

The flute sang again, soft and slow and gradually increasing in both volume and speed. Charlie reached for the goggles slung around his neck and secured them over his eyes, the boiler rumbling behind him as it built up steam. He stole a glance at his daughter, her body canted forward in anticipation. With the sounding of the start note, Charlie shot down the hill, wheels sparking. Phil pushed into the air with her powerful legs, wings spread.

As in any race of wheels against wings, strict rules and conditions ensured a fair outcome. A net slung thirty feet above the entire length of the racetrack kept the flyer low, preventing the use of altitude to circumvent changes in elevation. Beginning on a downhill stretch allowed the wheeled racer to get a faster start, the challenge being to maintain that lead once the flyer gained momentum. The long straightaway was the final means of evening the race. Since the flyer used body strength and the wheeled racer used steam, the flyer would need to maintain speed despite tiring muscles.

Charlie lost sight of his daughter when she rose into the air. The chugging of the steam engine nearly drowned out the enthusiastic cheers of the crowd lining both sides of the racetrack. He caught a glimpse of a young, dark-haired boy waving a green and grey flag and his breath hitched. Alan? Not possible. Alan was ten years dead, killed by an infection caused by the surgery to attach an improved right leg. Lorene had argued against the enhancement. There had been nothing wrong with his son's leg, unlike Charlie's, which had been destroyed in the chemical wars. His enhancements were necessary whereas Alan's were optional. But Charlie knew that the future belonged to the hybrids. His children would be strong.

The sounds of the crowd told him that Phil was gaining. He turned his face up and to the right. Strong wingbeats moved her along just under the net. She looked down and smiled, a cold triumphant smile that didn't reach her eyes. Then with an extra flap of her wings she was past him.

He grasped the handle on his left and pushed it forward, increasing both the amount of fuel and the temperature of the firebox. A burst of steam powered him forward and he began to close the distance. Charlie drew even with his daughter, sweat pouring off his face. A few drops slipped under the edge of his left goggle and blinded him. He shook his head to clear his vision and blinked rapidly. He moved the handle another couple of centimeters, praying that the engine still had something left. He caught up with his daughter and crept ahead.

The smell of the superheated steam brought back memories of Eliza, the daughter who'd adored him and wanted to be just like him. Charlie had basked in the attention and encouraged her ambitions, promising her the enhancements as soon as she was old enough. He'd been unprepared for her eagerness. She'd gone to an illegal enhancement clinic and survived the surgery, but perished when her steam engine malfunctioned, scalding her to death.

Eliza's death increased the distance between him and Lorene. Because Philomena was still young, Lorene stayed. But the marriage was effectively over. All he'd asked was that she not humiliate him. She couldn't even do that much.

The finish line was not yet in sight. If he could maintain this pace, Phil would soon begin to tire. But instead of tiring, she kept up, just a bit behind but well within reach. Then he lost sight of her. Had she dropped farther behind? A glance in the rear-view mirror showed her directly behind him. She'd moved into his slipstream and was drafting! A burst at the finish line would give her the win.

Charlie couldn't help the pride he felt at his daughter's strategy. During her time as his lieutenant, Phil had always come up with well-reasoned plans when other aides reacted emotionally. Only sixteen when she joined his staff, she'd listened and learned. Charlie had been considering stepping aside in her favor when Lorene had betrayed him. Now twenty-one, Phil had spent the two years since her mother's death training physically and mentally to topple him. Maybe after he won the race, he could also win back her service, if not her affection.

But first, the race. He thumbed the red button on the accelerator handle, waiting for the right moment. When her wings were fully raised in an upbeat, he pressed the button, releasing a jet of steam directly into her face. Phil shrieked and instinctively rose into the air. Her left wing hit the net and threw her off balance. She plummeted toward the ground, saving herself at the last minute by pushing off with her taloned feet and sweeping her powerful wings downward. Charlie watched her image shrink in his rear-view mirror and smiled. She was humiliated but unhurt. Well, her face might be blistered for a while, but she'd recover.

She was as formidable an opponent as she'd been valuable as an ally. She'd sacrificed her feet and the musculature of her back for increased strength and power. This was the one area she and her mother had disagreed upon. Lorene remained adamantly opposed to enhancements unless they were replacing non-functional parts.

He held the accelerator handle steady, stealing occasional glances in the mirror. He watched as the white shape began to grow larger. He'd underestimated her determination. And her strength. The needle of the engine's heat dial quivered in the red zone. If he pushed any harder, he risked an engine failure. Or an explosion. He spied the finish line on the horizon, but Phil was regaining lost ground. Careful not to get behind him again, she pulled alongside once more and turned her scalded face his way with a look of pure hatred.

A chill ran through Charlie's body, despite the heat from the steam engine. He pressed the handle forward. The engine screamed but responded. Somehow Phil kept up and the racers remained neck and neck, moving so fast it seemed the finish line was racing toward them rather than the other way.

With a mighty downbeat of her wings, Phil moved past him by a body length. Her talons trailed in the air just to his right, hazy sunlight reflecting off silver. The racers stayed in this arrangement for three beats of her wings before she screamed as a red stain spread across the left side of her back. Her left wing dropped to her side, useless. Her right wing continued its downward motion and pushed her body into a cartwheel. She tumbled across the rails in a flurry of white, her momentum sliding her forward in front of Charlie's wheels. He grabbed the brake handle and pulled with all his might, his instinct to protect his daughter overriding his lust for power.

Somehow, he slowed enough to allow Phil to roll off the tracks. He watched in the mirror as she lifted her head.

Relieved, he moved his gaze forward. A wall of flame obscured his vision. His top hat ignited and the smell of burning hair filled his nostrils as the fire spread. Charlie had become a rolling fireball speeding toward the crowd gathered at the finish line. He yanked on the brake, hot metal searing his palm. The handle snapped off. If he reached the finish line, hundreds would die with him. He pressed the button and dumped all the remaining coal into the firebox.

Charlie exploded well shy of the finish line, saving his people and earning the grudging respect of his daughter, the new Chief.

THE LOOKOUT

Colors churned and boiled in the sky, raw emotion painted on the horizon. Puffs of purple and black rolled together like a bruise, the colors of screaming and anguish. But only I saw them. I scrambled down the ladder and raced to the command center. Towering walls kept invaders at bay and darkened the courtyard.

My pounding feet on the crude wooden floorboards alerted General Webster. She looked up from maps spread across the table and nodded.

"Yes, Corporal?"

Major Hawk stood to her right, frowning at the interruption.

My hands shook as they formed the warning. "Screaming. From the south."

"Are you sure?" Her slow signing was accompanied by a yellow cloud of speech, the color of caution.

Major Hawk glanced at her impassive face and his frown cleared, but his lips remained pursed.

General Webster spoke the word and we signed it together, "Golett."

Her speech cloud darkened to a worried orange. Golett was a trading center with no real defenses. The unspoken agreement to leave merchants alone had been broken. The Major shook his head in denial. Angry puffs of dark blue left his mouth with every word. He had never learned to sign and covered his mouth, as usual, so I couldn't read his lips.

Deafness was not unusual in our nation-state of Arexico. Decades of war and the poisonous weapons used by both sides had affected generations. To bear a live child was a blessing. In my case, one sense had been lost but another had been gained.

The General gave me a sympathetic look.

"Take a scout team. Confirm the attack and report casualties, if possible." She mouthed calm, light green words while she signed. "Do not engage."

I delivered a snappy salute and turned to the door, catching Hawk's angry glare, safely delivered from his position behind her right shoulder.

The position of lookout was exclusive to the deaf because we would not be distracted from our task. General Webster had personally requested my assignment to her outpost. She'd heard about my "special gift" from my training officer. Not everyone was pleased at my arrival, however. Major Hawk doubted my gift, always looking for opportunities to prove my reports wrong. He has not been successful.

On my way to prepare for the scouting expedition, I wondered again how General Webster could be so blind. She was a fair and thoughtful commander, but she trusted the Major. He had made himself essential in planning military strategy. A vain and handsome man, he had also charmed his way into her bed. I often saw vivid pinks and corals swirling over her quarters during late night "briefings." The colors of desire, but not of love. Thank the Goddess.

I led a single file of horses and riders. Charcoal and amethyst clouds rolled high overhead, like beads on a string. After two days, the hearing scouts detected sounds to accompany the colors. But the clouds were getting smaller, the colors were getting lighter, and the screams were weakening. Slavery would be the fate of the less fortunate denizens of Golett—the survivors.

A swirling maroon mist hovered above a rocky area near the edge of the plateau overlooking the city. I put a finger to my lips and the flat of my hand toward the team. I crept toward the colorful mass and it shrunk, as if its creators could sense me. The rocks revealed a small cave, not much more than a slit, with four people pressed into the crease in a desperate effort to become invisible. Two of them were children, the small girl enclosed in the protective arms of an only slightly older boy. He pushed her behind him with a fierce expression and stepped forward. The woman's hand slipped off the boy's shoulder while an anxious crimson burst floated from her mouth. The silent man could barely stand, his right leg a bloody mess.

"Can you help us?" the boy signed. His small fingers were skilled.

"Did anyone else escape?" I didn't have to slow my signing for him.

He looked at the ground and shook his head, but I'd already seen the tears.

I waved the head scout over and signed orders to the only team member who spoke my language. He objected to the extra load on the horses, and the strain on our dwindling supplies, but I was the one in charge of this mission. He cupped his hands around his mouth to tell the rest of the team. A cobalt stream shot from his mouth, revealing his anger.

The boy raised his head to watch the color cloud rise and break apart. He met my eyes.

"I told you not to engage." General Webster's signing was choppy and abrupt, her lips pressed into a thin line. A halo of indigo formed over her head. She was as angry as I'd ever seen her. "Three more mouths to feed?"

The badly injured man, the children's father, died of a fever on the first day of the three it took us to return.

"The woman has valuable information about the attack," I signed. "And the other two are children. How could I leave them?"

The General's face softened, as I'd hoped, at the appeal. Children are rare and valued. I darted my eyes toward the smug Major, stationed as usual behind her. "May we speak privately, Ma'am?"

"That will be all, Major," she said, in a stream of commanding emerald.

The grin fell from his face. He saluted and marched from the room. I watched until the door closed behind him and turned back to General Webster.

"The boy," I signed. "He is like me."

Her eyes lit up. She ordered me to begin training him as a lookout.

After leaving the General's office, I led the small family—mother Janelle, girl Sarah, and boy Matthias—to a small room with a double bed, table, chair, and washbasin.

"I'm afraid this is the best we can offer," I signed.

"Thank you. Very generous, Corporal," Janelle said, so upset she forgot to sign but I read her lips.

"Please, call me Susannah," I signed, then rested a re-assuring hand on her arm. She gave me a weak smile. She looked overwhelmed.

"Ma and Sarah can have the bed and I'll take the floor," said Matthias. He took his mother's hand. "Don't worry, Ma. We're safe now." He gave me a challenging glare, as if daring me to argue.

I explained the settlement routine to them, letting them know when meals were served and what work was expected from the residents. I signed slowly; Janelle and Sarah knew sign language but were not as adept as Matthias. The mention of the school available for the children earned a smile from little Sarah and a frown from Matthias.

"I don't have time for school," the boy signed. "I'm head of the family now and should be given a job."

"As it turns out, we do have a job in mind for you."

When I told the General the boy was like me, it wasn't entirely true. Matthias, should his training succeed, would be more valuable than me. My gift cost me both my hearing and power of speech. I cannot produce any sound at all. Matthias has only paid with his hearing. He has a voice and thus can communicate with everyone instead of just those who have signing skills.

Matthias grudgingly agreed to attend school in the mornings. I scheduled his training for the afternoons. He shadowed me on my duties, paying close attention to both my words and deeds. He was an excellent student. Scanning the horizon for sounds was a game to him. His young eyes detected distant sounds before my older eyes did. Our shared skill bound us—he became the younger brother I never had.

Every third week, I was assigned the night shift. During those weeks, Matthias shadowed Private Evans in the afternoon. He grumbled to me at first, but eventually got used to her. According to Evans, he was focused and intent on practicing his skills.

Matthias adored the General, and she was fond of him. She often invited the boy into her office where he sat quietly, watching the comings and goings. The other soldiers grew so used to his presence he became invisible. Invisible to all except Major Hawk, who resented anyone who got close to the General. He tried unsuccessfully to have the boy and his family moved to smaller quarters, claiming their room was needed for soldiers. Matthias quickly learned not to be caught alone by the Major or else suffer a clout about the ears.

Matthias' small stature and silence allowed him to move through the settlement almost unnoticed. In this way, he was privy to many of the secrets and petty plots that bubbled up in any small society, especially one under constant threat of attack. He shared his discoveries with me at the beginning of each shift and we usually had a good laugh. Sometimes, however, he overheard a scheme which could endanger everyone, settlers and soldiers alike. In those cases, I had a quiet word with the plotters (using a neutral interpreter if necessary) and warned them off. If they didn't listen, the alternative would be a report to the General and the risk of expulsion from the sheltering walls of the camp. And if the plotters were soldiers, they could face much worse punishment. So far, the warnings had worked.

As clever and resourceful as Matthias was, I still worried about him when I wasn't there. Major Hawk's dislike of the boy had infected his subordinates and created more than one enemy. So, when Matthias admired a small, moonstone-encrusted dagger that had belonged to my father, I gave it to him without a second thought. Knowing he could defend himself eased my mind. My father would have approved.

But one evening I was preparing for my watch shift when Matthias came to my quarters in tears, his brow furrowed with worry.

"What's wrong?" I asked, urging him to sit.

"The Major," he signed rapidly.

Matthias had discovered a dangerous plot, led by Major Hawk, to convince the rest of the officers that the General was unfit for duty. He had forged her signature on orders to send a regiment into battle without sufficient cover or arms. After the doomed regiment was defeated, he planned to have her court-martialed. Of course, he was next in command. Four other officers had been enlisted in the scheme.

"When does he plan to move forward?"

"I don't know!" Matthias' signing was panicked and jerky, a tangerine mist of worry rose above his head. "We must warn the General."

"Not yet," I responded, thinking hard about how to convince General Webster that her right-hand man (and lover) would betray her. "I'll do it first thing in the morning."

But morning was too late.

Later that moonlit autumn night, a deep violet scream boiled up from the General's quarters. I rushed from my post to find General Webster in her nightclothes, her mouth filled with the color of confusion and anger. Major Hawk stood over a small body, my father's dagger in his hand. Umber puffs of lies surrounded his head.

A soundless deep blue cry of rage erupted from my mouth as I rushed the Major, slamming into his back and driving him to the ground. Although he was larger, I was quicker. I wrested the dagger from his hand and plunged it into his chest again and again, my only thought revenge. The General pulled me away and I stumbled toward Matthias and cradled him in my arms as blood bubbled from his poor slashed throat. The strong arms of soldiers dragged me away from the small, crumpled body. I was locked in my quarters to stare numbly at the ceiling. Realization sunk in. I had murdered a senior officer. I would be hanged. I dropped my face into my hands and wept. For Matthias. For myself.

General Webster came to see me the next morning, accompanied by two armed guards. She told them to stand outside the room, entered, and closed the door.

"Corporal Lee. Susannah. How are you?" She signed slowly, mouthing words accompanied by a soothing seafoam cloud.

I hung my head, remembering Matthias' last gasp. "Why?" I signed rapidly. "Why did Major Hawk kill him? He was a child!"

"Matthias had come to me to tell me of a plot led by Major Hawk."

"I told him to leave it alone, that I would tell you today." I rubbed my face and looked at her before continuing. "He loved you."

She dropped her hands in her lap and sighed, looking pensive. Her ruby exhalation revealed that she returned the boy's love. "Matthias had just warned me of the plot when I heard Hawk's footsteps." She blushed. "We had arranged to meet..."

"I know about you and the Major," I signed, my face impassive.

The General shook her head. "A lapse in judgement. I can see that now." She paused, then began signing again. "I hid the boy in the clothes cubby until I could get rid of Hawk. I needed more time to think about what to do. But as soon as Hawk touched me, Matthias became enraged and flew out of hiding, waving a dagger and accusing the Major of treason. It happened so quickly. Hawk easily disarmed the boy and cut his throat, swearing the child was trying to attack me and that he'd saved my life."

My heart sank. If I hadn't given Matthias the dagger, he might still be alive. My attempt to protect him had killed him.

"While I cannot condone what you did," she continued, "I do thank you for saving me the trouble of a court-martial for Major Hawk."

General Webster glanced at the closed door, then crouched in front of my cot and signed rapidly. "Mark what I say. You are confined to quarters until the investigation is complete. Your testimony will match mine. Major Hawk assaulted me. Matthias bravely came to my defense and lost his life. You ran into the room and saw what had happened. While you were trying to assist the boy, I disarmed Hawk and killed him with his own weapon. Do you understand?"

"We have the orders with the forged signature!" I shook my head. "You can't take the blame for my actions."

"This way is better," she said. "With the power of my position, any further investigation will be dropped. Even though your actions are justifiable, the repercussions of killing a superior officer will follow you."

I reluctantly agreed.

The investigation went just as the General planned. Hawk's co-conspirators were called to testify. With the forged document as evidence and without their leader, they had no defense. Major Bert Simmons was hanged for treason. His corpse was moved to the gate to serve as an example. For two days birds and insects devoured his soft body parts. When the smell became too much, his remains were thrown outside the gate to feed the larger scavengers. The other three conspirators were reduced in rank but allowed to live. All pledged fervent loyalty.

The General delivered a wondrous eulogy at Matthias' funeral. Her words would have made him blush. I sat between Janelle and Sarah, hands linked as we all three wept, the air silver with sorrow.

I continue as the sole gifted lookout for the settlement. Another like me has not been discovered.

But in tribute to Matthias, I remain hopeful.

STORY NOTES

As a beginning writer, if I was given a prompt or theme to write to, any ideas that may have been lurking in my subconscious fled as if pursued by zombies. Fortunately I overcame that fear, and now prompts and themes are the source of many of my stories. The combination of a prompt and a deadline have pushed me to produce some of my best work. I also draw inspiration from the weirdness of daily life and my twisted way of thinking. The stories in this collection spring from both sources.

"Inheritance" I wrote this story for submission to a Medusa-themed anthology. It did not make the cut. After sending it out to a couple more times, it found a home in the *Sirens Call* ezine. I enjoyed the challenge of writing a flash piece, one of my first, and never mentioning the name "Medusa" in the story. The story focused instead upon her descendants.

"Hecate's Promise" This is the first of four previously unpublished stories to appear in this collection. I wrote it for a Gothic Fantasy anthology (from Flame Tree Press) focusing on moon deities and legends. It did not make the cut. (Are you sensing a pattern here?) But the competition was fierce and I believed in my story. "Be careful what you wish for" is one of my favorite tropes. I learned a lot about the goddess Hecate in the writing process, and am happy to include her story on the menu.

"A Delicate Matter" This is my first story in a historical setting. It opened the door to many more, since I enjoy research and love the ability to strip characters of 24/7 communications. It was written in response to a prompt (cursed object), but the ring is real—an antique Victorian ring I inherited from my mother. The story represented the lone genre fiction in a sea of literary fiction in the anthology in which it was published.

"The Tinker's Gift" Another story written for a specific submission call (mirrors). Say it with me; it did not make the cut. Living in Virginia, I am surrounded by Civil War history. Mrs. Forsythe's mansion/field hospital was inspired by The Exchange Hotel and Civil War Museum, less than fifteen miles from my home. Bartley Penfold is the tinker referenced in the title. He is flattered to have been revived to serve as maitre'd for this collection and promises to behave himself.

"Oyster Hunt" The prompt was plant horror. I subbed the story twice, with the second market (Dark Recesses

Press) accepting and publishing it. This was great fun to write, and I spent many happy hours researching mycology to come up with something both horrible and feasible.

"Family Tree" A previously unpublished story. It was inspired by the memorials that crop up on sharp turns, and sometimes on ruler straight sections of roads. I wondered how the property owners of the locations dealt with them, and for how long. And what about the tree? The first draft of this story was written in 2018. It has evolved over the years through seven drafts and nineteen submissions, garnering some personalized rejections and near misses in the process. This story has grown with me as a writer, and I'm proud to add it to the menu.

"Amazing Patsy" My first professional sale. The prompt was cryptids, but the toads aren't nearly as scary as Patsy. Little girls are deceptively sweet. I enjoyed finding Granny's voice and making the setting come to life. The story was well-received at my first StokerCon reading in 2019. A reprint submission made it to the final round at Podcastle, but alas, did not cross the finish line.

"An Echo of Murder" Another story written from a prompt (evil child). This is gorier than my usual fiction, but it was fun to stretch my writing muscles by making the gore integral to the story instead of thrown in for effect. After being published in the Carnage House ezine, a reprint was selected for the paperback anthology, *The Best of Carnage House, Year One.*

"Salt Pork" A previously unpublished story, and my most challenging prompt—necrophilia! After much apprehension and dread, this story turned out to be one of my favorites. The necrophilia is a small part of the larger story. I enjoyed writing it so much that I carried the characters (pirates and mermaids, what's not to like?) and setting from this story to the next one.

"Silent Maidens" Haunted vessels was the prompt, so using the pirate ship from "Salt Pork" was a no-brainer. Since Mr. Cameron disappeared into the deep in the last tale, this story picks up with the sole survivor of the sinking, Daniel the cook. I got to play on the high seas once again and enjoyed bringing the saga of the *Phoenix* full circle. This story is the last of the previously unpublished works on the menu.

"The Wages of Sin" A kaiju story. I took a wild boar (which are huge under normal circumstances), added in a bit of science gone wrong, and topped it off with some good old-fashioned workplace pilferage. Mix well, allow to grow, and we have the story of Yevgeny Petrovitch, just trying to earn a living to support his family.

"A Mischief in Gordonsville" This story came from my first ever invitation to submit an anthology. All proceeds from *Dark Corners of the Old Dominion* benefit Scares That Care, a wonderful Virginia charity. The tale is set in the same building (The Exchange Hotel) that inspired "A Tinker's Gift." In researching Civil War hospitals, I discovered that rats were a constant problem. A super smart rat, a touch of reincarnation, and I was off and running.

"The Succession" My first published story. It won third prize in the Blue Ridge Writers 2017 writing competition, earning me $25 and publication in the BRW anthology (once again, the only genre fiction in the antho). The story was inspired by a large knothole in a tree that I drove by every day on my way into town. I wondered what kind of creature could live there, and Orrla, queen of the pixies was born.

"Shiny Objects" I love garden gnome statues. Four of them graced my flowerbed at one time. Since one of my garden gnomes had a pot of gold, the story took a riches-obsessed gnome and turned him into a grave robber. A rookie detective made the mistake of trying to do his job and got in the way of the gnome and his family. But the gnomes weren't monsters—they were nice to his dog!

"Wheels Against Wings" The submission call was for stories inspired by rock songs of the 50's, 60's, and 70's. First, I had to pick the song (Locomotive Breath by Jethro Tull, 1971), then be careful not to quote lyrics or otherwise anger the copyright gods (or their lawyers). If you look at the lyrics, you'll be able to see how I interpreted them to create the story of Charlie and his daughter. This was also my first attempt at steampunk, and I'm pretty happy with how it turned out.

"The Lookout" This story was born in 2018 at Borderlands Boot Camp. We were given a first line late Friday night and had to write a story to be read aloud to all the campers and instructors on Sunday morning (Fun fact—the first draft was read aloud by the guest author that weekend, the great Peter Straub). My line was "A screaming comes across the sky." (from *Gravity's Rainbow* by Thomas Pynchon). The only way I could imagine seeing a screaming was through color synesthesia. After many revisions and submissions, I'm pleased the story finally found a home in *Space and Time* magazine (a bucket list market).

CONTENT WARNINGS

When the genre is horror, content warnings can seem unnecessary. However, as a writer I aim to entertain, not traumatize. So I've included content warnings only if the subject matter either falls outside the norm for the genre, or if it could cause distress to those who have experienced or otherwise been adversely affected by it.

"A Delicate Matter" – Infanticide

"Oyster Hunt" – Animal death

"An Echo of Murder" – Animal cruelty

"Salt Pork" – Necrophilia

"A Mischief in Gordonsville" – Desecration of the dead

"Shiny Objects" – Desecration of the dead

ACKNOWLEDGEMENTS

When I began writing, short fiction called to me and it remains my first love. Over the years, I've had quite a few short stories published. This collection includes twelve of them. However, there are also some stories near and dear to my heart that have yet to catch the eye of an editor or publisher. I've included four of those in this collection.

Structuring a collection is a challenge—what stories to include, the theme, how to order them, etc. A multi-course meal contains a variety of foods, so I decided a menu structure would work for the variety of stories contained herein. Adding one of my favorite fictional creations, Bartley Penfold, as a guide gave life to the selections and provided a new role for the itinerant tinker.

None of these stories would exist without much study, critique, rewriting, and many submissions before finally being accepted for publication. I took courses and workshops from WriterHouse (a non-profit writing center),

Borderlands Boot Camp, Moanaria's Fright Club, and the Horror Writers Association, all of which helped me sand down the rough parts and learn to be a real writer.

Getting the stories over the finish line to publication wouldn't have been possible without the insightful feedback from my writing group, the Monday Night Write Club. Special thanks to Terry Emery, Ken Godfrey, Larry Hinkle, Tom Deady, Christa Carmen, and Mary Ann Back for their encouragement and support.

I'm grateful to Ruth Anna Evans, the talented cover artist for this collection. She took my vision and made it real—better than I had imagined. The cover captures the mood and vibe I was hoping for. Mr. Penfold is pleased.

Thanks to my family for their love during this long journey—John Williams, Bill Bowers, David Bowers, Steve Bowers, Chris Ambrose, and Lesley Ambrose. And I couldn't have done it without all the dogs who provided moral support, sloppy kisses, and total acceptance throughout the years.

Valerie B. Williams
September 2025
Charlottesville, Virginia

Photo by Alysa Foytik, PuraPhoto

Valerie B. Williams' short speculative fiction has been published in over twenty anthologies and magazines. Her debut novel, a story of supernatural suspense titled "The Vanishing Twin," was released in October 2024. She is an Active member of the Horror Writers Association (HWA). Valerie spins twisty tales from her home in central Virginia, which she shares with her very patient husband and equally patient Golden Retriever. When not writing, she can be found reading and drinking either tea or wine, depending on the time of day.